Brighton Beach Memoirs

by *Neil Simon*

SAMUEL FRENCH, INC.
45 WEST 25TH STREET   NEW YORK
7623 SUNSET BOULEVARD   HOLL
LONDON

ISBN 0 573 61941 7   Printed in U.S.A.   #298

ALVIN THEATRE

UNDER THE DIRECTION OF THE MESSRS. NEDERLANDER

EMANUEL AZENBERG, WAYNE M. ROGERS, RADIO CITY MUSIC HALL PRODUCTIONS
in association with
CENTER THEATRE GROUP/AHMANSON

present

NEIL SIMON'S

BRIGHTON BEACH MEMOIRS

Starring (in alphabetical order)

MATTHEW BRODERICK   **ELIZABETH FRANZ**   **PETER MICHAEL GOETZ**

MANDY INGBER   **ŽELJKO IVANEK**   **JODI THELEN**   **JOYCE VAN PATTEN**

Setting designed by   Costumes designed by   Lighting designed by
DAVID MITCHELL   **PATRICIA ZIPPRODT**   **THARON MUSSER**

Directed By

GENE SAKS

The Producers and Theatre Management are Members
of The League of New York Theatres and Producers, Inc.

CAST
(in order of appearance)

Eugene .... MATTHEW BRODERICK

Blanche .... JOYCE VAN PATTEN

Kate .... ELIZABETH FRANZ

Laurie .... MANDY INGBER

Nora .... JODI THELEN

Stanley .... ŽELJKO IVANEK

Jack .... PETER MICHAEL GOETZ

SYNOPSIS OF SCENES
ACT I
Brighton Beach, Brooklyn, New York
September, 1937—6:30 p.m.
ACT II
Wednesday, a week later.
About 6:45 in the evening.
STANDBYS
Standbys never substitute for a listed player unless a specific
announcement is made at the time of the performance.
For Kate and Blanche—DONNA HALEY; for Nora—ROBIN MORSE; for Eugene and
Stanley—TIMOTHY BUSFIELD; for Laurie—PAMELA SEGALL;
for Jack—STEFAN GIERASCH; for Stanley—J. PATRICK BREEN.

Brighton Beach Memoirs

ACT ONE

Brighton Beach, N.Y. September, 1937.

A wooden frame house, not too far from the beach. It is a lower middle income area inhabited mostly by Jews, Irish and Germans.

The entrance to the house is at stage R., *a small porch and two steps up that lead to the front door.*

Inside we see the dining room and living room area. Another door leads to the kitchen . . . A flight of stairs leads up to three small bedrooms. Unseen are two other bedrooms. A hallway leads to other rooms . . .

It's about six-thirty P.M. and the late September sun is sinking fast.

AT RISE: *KATE JEROME, about 40 years old is setting up for dinner. Her sister, BLANCHE MORTON, 38, is working at a sewing machine.*

LAURIE MORTON, aged 13, is lying on the sofa, reading a book.

Outside on the grass is EUGENE JEROME, almost but not quite 15. He is wearing knickers, a shirt and tie, a faded and torn sweater, Keds sneakers and a blue baseball cap. He has a beaten and worn baseball glove on his left hand and in his right hand he holds a ball that is so old and battered, it is ready to fall apart.

He stands on an imaginary pitcher's mound, facing stage L. *He looks back over his shoulder to an imaginary runner on second, then back over to the "batter." Then he winds up and pitches, hitting an offstage wall.*

EUGENE. One out, a man on second, bottom of the seventh, two balls, no strikes . . . Ruffing checks the runner on second, gets the sign from Dickey, Ruffing stretches, Ruffing pitches. (*He throws the ball.*) . . . Caught the inside corner, steerike one! Atta baby! No hitter up there. (*He retrieves the ball.*) One out, a man on second, bottom of the seventh, two balls one strike . . . Ruffing checks the runner on second, gets the sign from Dickey, Ruffing stretches, Ruffing pitches—(*He throws the ball.*) Low and outside, ball three. Come on, Red! Make him a hitter! No batter up there. In there all the time, Red.

BLANCHE. (*stops sewing*) Kate, please. My head is splitting.

KATE. I told that boy a hundred and nine times. (*She yells out.*) Eugene! Stop banging the wall!

EUGENE. (*calls out*) In a minute, Ma! This is for the World Series! (*back to his game*) One out, a man on second, bottom of the seventh, three balls, one strike . . . Ruffing stretches, Ruffing pitches—(*He throws ball.*) Oh, no! High and outside, JoJo Moore walks! First and second and Mel Ott lopes up to the plate . . .

BLANCHE. (*stops again*) Can't he do that someplace else?

KATE. I'll break his arm, that's where he'll do it. (*calls out*) Eugene, I'm not going to tell you again. Do you hear me?

EUGENE. It's the last batter, Mom. Mel Ott is up. It's a crucial moment in World Series history.

KATE. Your Aunt Blanche has a splitting headache.

BLANCHE. I don't want him to stop playing. It's just the banging.

LAURIE. (*looks up from her book*) He always does it when I'm studying. I have a big test in history tomorrow.

EUGENE. One pitch, Mom? I think I can get him to pop up. I have my stuff today.

KATE. Your father will give you plenty of stuff when he comes home! You hear!

EUGENE. Alright! Alright!

KATE. I want you inside *now!* Put out the water glasses.

BLANCHE. I can do that.

KATE. Why? Is his arm broken? (*yells out again*) And I don't want any back talk, you hear? (*She goes back to kitchen.*)

EUGENE. (*Slams ball into his glove angrily. Then he cups his hand, making a megaphone out of it and announces to the grandstands:*) . . . "Attention, ladeees and gentlemen! Today's game will be delayed because of my Aunt Blanche's headache . . ."

KATE. Blanche, that's enough sewing today. That's all I need is for you to go blind.

BLANCHE. I just have this one edge to finish . . . Laurie, darling, help your Aunt Kate with the dishes.

LAURIE. Two more pages, alright, Ma? I have to finish the Macedonian Wars.

KATE. Always studying, that one. She's gonna have some head on her shoulders. (*calls out from kitchen*) Eugene!!

EUGENE. I'm coming.

KATE. And wash your hands.

EUGENE. They're clean. I'm wearing a glove. (*He throws ball into glove again . . . then he looks out front and addresses the audience.*) . . . I hate my name! . . . Eugene Morris Jerome . . . It is the second worst name ever given to a male child . . . The first worst is Haskell Fleischmann . . . How am I ever going to play for the Yankees with a name like Eugene Morris Jerome? . . . You have to be a Joe . . . or a Tony . . . Or Frankie . . .

If only I was born Italian . . . All the best Yankees are Italian . . . My mother makes spaghetti with ketchup, what chance do I have? (*He slams the ball into glove again.*)

LAURIE. I'm almost through, Ma.

BLANCHE. Alright, darling. Don't get up too quickly.

KATE. (*to LAURIE*) You have better color today, sweetheart. Did you get a little sun this morning?

LAURIE. I walked down to the beach.

BLANCHE. Very slowly, I hope?

LAURIE. Yes, Ma.

BLANCHE. That's good.

EUGENE. (*He's been listening . . . then turns to audience again.*) . . . She gets all this special treatment because the doctors say she has kind of a flutter in her heart . . . I got hit with a baseball right in the back of the skull, I saw two of everything for a week and I still had to carry a block of ice home every afternoon . . . Girls are treated like queens . . . Maybe that's what I should have been born . . . An Italian girl . . .

KATE. (*picks up a sweat sock from the floor*) *Eugene!!*

EUGENE. *What??*

KATE. How many times have I told you not to leave your things around the house?

EUGENE. A hundred and nine.

KATE. What?

EUGENE. You said yesterday, "I told you a hundred and nine times not to leave your things around the house."

BLANCHE. Don't be fresh to your mother, Gene!

EUGENE. (*to audience*) Was I fresh? I swear to God, that's what she said to me yesterday . . . One day I'm going to put all this in a book or a play . . . I'm going to be a writer like Ring Lardner or somebody . . . that's if things don't work out first with the Yankees . . . or the Cubs . . . or the Red Sox . . . or maybe possibly the Tigers . . . If I get down to the St. Louis Browns, then I'll definitely be a writer.

LAURIE. Mom, can I have a glass of lemonade?

BLANCHE. It'll spoil your dinner, darling.

KATE. A small glass, it couldn't hurt her.

BLANCHE. Alright. In a minute, angel.

KATE. I'll get it. I'm in the kitchen anyway.

EUGENE. (to audience) Can you believe that? . . . She'd better have a bad heart or I'm going to kill her one day . . . (He gets up to cross into the house, then stops on the porch steps and turns to the audience again . . . confidentially.) Listen, I hope you don't repeat this to anybody . . . What I'm telling you are my secret memoirs . . . It's called, "The Unbelievable, Fantastic and Completely Private Thoughts of I, Eugene Morris Jerome, in this, the fifteenth year of his life, in the year nineteen hundred and thirty-seven, in the community of Brighton Beach, Borough of Brooklyn, Kings County, City of New York, Empire State of the American Nation—"

KATE. (comes out of kitchen with a glass of lemonade and one roller skate) A roller skate? On my kitchen floor? Do you want me dead, is that what you want?

EUGENE. (rushes into the house) I didn't leave it there.

KATE. No? Then who? Laurie? Aunt Blanche? Did you ever see them on skates? . . . (holds out skate) Take this upstairs . . . Come here!

EUGENE. (approaches, holding the back of his head) Don't hit my skull, I have a concussion.

KATE. What would you tell your father if he came home and I was dead on the kitchen floor?

EUGENE. I'd say, "Don't go in the kitchen, Pa!"

KATE. (*She swings at him, he ducks and she misses.*) Get upstairs! And don't come down with dirty hands.

(*EUGENE goes up the stairs. He turns to the audience:*)

EUGENE. You see why I want to write all this down? . . . In case I grow up all twisted and warped, the world will know why.

BLANCHE. (*still sewing*) He's a boy. He's young. You should be glad he's healthy and active. Before the doctors found out what Laurie had, she was the same way.

KATE. Never. Girls are different. When you and I were girls, we kept the house spotless. It was Ben and Ezra who drove Momma crazy.

(*We see EUGENE upstairs, enter his room and take out a notebook and pencil and lay down on his bed, making a new entry in his "memoirs."*)

KATE. . . . I've always been like that. I have to have things clean. Just like Momma. The day they packed up and left the house in Russia, she cleaned the place from top to bottom. She said, "No matter what the Cossacks did to us, when they broke into her house, they would have respect for the Jews."

LAURIE. Who were the Cossacks?

KATE. The same filthy bunch as live across the street.

LAURIE. Across the street? You mean the Murphys?

KATE. *All* of them.

LAURIE. The Murphys are Russian?

BLANCHE. The mother is nice. She's been very sweet to me.

KATE. Her windows are so filthy, I thought she had black curtains hanging inside.

BLANCHE. I was in their house. It was very neat. *Nobody* could be as clean as you.

KATE. What business did you have in their house?

BLANCHE. She invited me for tea.

KATE. To meet that drunken son of hers?

BLANCHE. No. Just the two of us.

KATE. I'm living here seven years, she never invited *me* for tea. Because she knows your situation. I know their kind. Remember what Momma used to tell us. Stay on your own side of the street. That's what they have gutters for. (*She goes back into the kitchen.*)

EUGENE. (*writing, says aloud*) "That's-what-they-have-gutters-for" . . . (*to audience*) If my mother knew I was writing all this down, she would stuff me like one of her chickens . . . I'd better explain what she meant by Aunt Blanche's "situation" . . . You see, her husband, Uncle Dave, died six years ago from . . . (*He looks around.*) . . . this thing . . . They never say the word. They always whisper it. It was—(*He whispers.*)—Cancer! . . . I think they're afraid if they said it out loud, God would say, "I HEARD THAT! YOU SAID THE DREAD DISEASE! (*He points finger down.*) JUST FOR THAT, I SMITE YOU DOWN WITH IT!!" . . . There are some things that grown-ups just won't discuss . . . For example, my grandfather. He died from—(*He whispers.*)—Diptheria! . . . Anyway, after Uncle Dave died, he left Aunt Blanche with no money. Not even insurance . . . And she couldn't support herself because she has—(*He whispers.*) Asthma . . . So my big-hearted mother insisted we take her and her kids in to live with us. So they broke up our room into two small rooms and me and my brother Stan live on this side, and Laurie and her sister Nora live on the other side. My father thought it would just be tem-

porary but it's been three and a half years so far and I
think because of Aunt Blanche's situation, my father is
developing—(*He whispers.*)—High blood pressure!

(*He resumes his writing. KATE comes out of the kitchen
    with a pitcher of lemonade. She crosses to LAU-
    RIE.*)

KATE. Have some more lemonade, dear.
LAURIE. (*sits up*) Thank you, Aunt Kate.
BLANCHE. Drink it slowly.
LAURIE. I am.
KATE. (*looks at BLANCHE*) Blanche, that's enough
already. Since seven o'clock this morning.
BLANCHE. I was just stopping.
KATE. You'll sew your fingers together.
BLANCHE. It's getting dark anyway. (*She stops, sits
back, rubs eyes.*) I think I need new glasses.
LAURIE. Our teacher said you should change them
every two years.
KATE. (*to BLANCHE*) Would it kill you to put a
light on?
BLANCHE. I don't have to run up electric bills. I owe
you and Jack enough as it is.
KATE. Have I asked you for anything? You see
anybody starving around here? If I go hungry, you'll
give me something from your plate.
BLANCHE. Kate! I'm going to pay you and Jack back
someday. I don't know when, but I keep my word.
KATE. From your lips to the Irish Sweepstakes . . .
Go in and taste the soup. See if it needs salt.
(*BLANCHE goes into kitchen.*)
LAURIE. Should I put out the water glasses or is
Eugene going to do it?

(*EUGENE, having heard, slams his "memoirs" shut
  angrily. KATE yells up.*)

KATE. EUGENE! . . . It's the last time I'm going to
tell you! (*to LAURIE*) Just do the napkins, darling.
(*KATE goes into kitchen. LAURIE gets up and starts to
set out napkins. EUGENE sits up on his bed.*)

EUGENE. (*to audience*) Because of her "condition," I
have to do twice as much work around here . . . Boy, if
I could just make the Yankees, I'd be in St. Petersburg
this winter . . . (*He starts out and down the stairs.*) Her
sister Nora isn't too bad. She's sixteen. I don't mind her
much. (*He is downstairs by now.*) At least she's not too
bad to look at. (*He starts taking glasses down from
open cupboard.*) To be absolutely honest, this is the
year I started noticing girls that weren't too bad to look
at . . . Nora started developing about eight months ago
. . . I have the exact date written in my diary.

(*Suddenly we hear a voice. It is NORA.*)

NORA. Mom! Laurie! Aunt Kate! (*We see NORA, an
absolutely lovely sixteen and a half year old girl, with a
developed chest, bound across the front steps and into
the house. She is bubbling over with enthusiasm.*) I've
got incredible news, everybody!!

EUGENE. Hi, Nora!

NORA. Eugene! My sweet adorable handsome cousin!
Wait'll I tell you what's happened to me. (*She throws
her arms around him, hugs him close and kisses his
cheek. Then rushes into the other room to LAURIE.*)
I'm fainting! I'm absolutely fainting!

EUGENE. (*still stunned from the hug, turns to the audience*) . . . I felt her chest! . . . When she grabbed me,
I felt my first chest.

NORA. I can't believe this whole day!

LAURIE. What happened?

NORA. Where's Mom? Aunt Kate? I have to tell everyone. (*She rushes to the kitchen door.*) Everybody inside for the big news!

(*KATE and BLANCHE comes out from the kitchen. KATE is mashing potatoes in a pot.*

KATE. What's all the excitement?

BLANCHE. You're all red in the face.

NORA. Sit down, Mom, because I don't want you fainting on the floor.

KATE. Sit down, Blanche.

LAURIE. Mom, sit down. (*BLANCHE sits.*)

NORA. You too, Aunt Kate. Okay. Is everybody ready?

LAURIE. Stop dragging it out. The suspense is *killing* me.

BLANCHE. Don't say things like that, Laurie.

KATE. (*to others*) Can I hear what the girl has to say? . . . (*to NORA*) Go ahead, darling.

NORA. (*a little breathless*) Okay! Here goes! . . . I'm going to be in a Broadway show! (*They look at her in a stunned silence.*) It's a musical called *Abracadabra* . . . This man, Mr. Beckman, he's a producer, came to our dancing class this afternoon and he picked out three girls. We have to be at the Hudson Theater on Monday morning at ten o'clock to audition for the dance director. But on the way out he took me aside and said the job was good as mine. I have to call him tomorrow. I may have to go into town to talk to him about it. They start rehearsing a week from Monday and then it goes to Philadelphia, Wilmington and Washington . . . and then it comes to New York the second week in December. There are nine big musical numbers and there's going to be a big tank on the stage that you can see through and the big finale all takes place with the entire cast all under water . . . I mean, can you believe it? I'm going to be in a Broadway show, Momma! (*They are all still stunned.*)

BLANCHE. (*to KATE*) What is she talking about?

KATE. Do I know? Am I her mother?

LAURIE. How can you be in a show? Don't you have to sing and act?

NORA. I can sing.

LAURIE. No, you can't.

NORA. A little.

LAURIE. No, you can't.

NORA. I can carry a *tune*.

LAURIE. No, you can't.

NORA. Well, I probably won't have to. They're just looking for dancers.

LAURIE. On Broadway you have to sing and act.

NORA. How do *you* know? You never saw a Broadway show.

BLANCHE. Did you tell him how old you were?

NORA. He didn't ask me.

BLANCHE. He didn't ask if you were sixteen?

NORA. He just asked me to audition. My God, isn't anybody excited?

EUGENE. I am. It's the most fantastic thing I ever heard.

NORA. Thanks, Eugene. I'm glad somebody's excited.

EUGENE. (*turns to audience*) My God! I'll be sleeping right next door to a *showgirl!*

BLANCHE. How can you go to Philadelphia? What about school?

NORA. School? Momma, this is a Broadway show. This is what I want to do with my life. Algebra and English isn't going to help me on the stage.

LAURIE. *Aren't?*

NORA. Will you stay out of this!

BLANCHE. You mean not finish school? Not get a diploma? . . . Do you know how hard it is today for a girl to get a good job without a high school diploma?

NORA. But I've *got* a job. And I'll be making more money than *ten* girls with diplomas.

LAURIE. You don't have it yet. You still have to audition.

NORA. It's as good as mine. Mr. Beckman told me.

BLANCHE. And what if you, God forbid, broke a leg? . . . Or got heavy . . . How long do you think they'll keep you? Dancing is just for a few years. A diploma is forever. I know. I never had one. I know how hard it is to find a decent job. Aunt Kate knows. Tell her, Kate.

KATE. It's very hard.

NORA. Then why did you send me to dancing school for three years? Why do I spend two hours a day on a subway, four days a week after school, with money that you make going half blind over a broken sewing machine? Why, Momma?

BLANCHE. . . . Because it's my pleasure . . . Because I know how you love it . . . Because you asked me.

NORA. Then I'm asking you something else, Momma. Let me do something for *you* now. I could be making almost sixty dollars a week. Maybe even more . . . In two years when I get out of high school, I wouldn't make that much with a *college* diploma.

BLANCHE. (*takes a deep breath*) . . . I can't think now. It's almost dinner time. Uncle Jack will be home soon. We'll discuss it later. (*She gets up.*)

NORA. I have to know *now,* Momma. I have to call Mr. Beckman and let him know if I can go to the audition on Monday . . . At least let me audition. Let me find out first if they think I'm good enough . . . Please don't say no until Monday. (*They all look at BLANCHE. She looks down at her hands.*)

EUGENE. (*turns out to audience*) . . . It was a tense moment for everybody . . . I love tense moments! . . . Especially when I'm not the one they're all tense about. (*He turns back and looks at BLANCHE.*)

BLANCHE. . . . Well, God knows we can use the money. We all owe Aunt Kate and Uncle Jack enough as it is . . . I think they have as much say in this as I do . . . How do you feel about it, Kate?

KATE. (*shrugs*) Me? I never voted before in my life, why should I start with my own family? . . . I have to heat up the potatoes. (*She goes off to the kitchen.*)

BLANCHE. Then we'll leave it up to Uncle Jack. We'll let him make the decision. (*She starts for kitchen.*)

NORA. Why, Momma? I love him but he's not my father.

BLANCHE. Because I need help . . . Because I don't always know what the right thing to do is . . . Because I say so, that's why. (*She exits into kitchen. LAURIE and EUGENE stand there staring at the forlorn NORA.*)

EUGENE. . . . Eugene M. Jerome of New York casts one vote for "yes." (*NORA looks up at him, breaks into tears and runs out of the room and up the stairs. LAURIE follows her up. EUGENE turns out to audience:*) . . . What I'm about to tell you next, is so secret and private, that I've left instructions for my memoirs not to be opened until thirty years after my death . . . I, Eugene M. Jerome, have committed a mortal sin by lusting after my cousin Nora . . . I can tell you all this now because I'll be dead when you're reading it . . . If I had my choice between a tryout with the Yankees — and actually seeing her bare breasts for two and a half seconds, I would have some serious thinking to do . . . (*KATE comes out of the kitchen.*)

KATE. I need bread.

EUGENE. (*turns quickly*) What?

KATE. I don't have enough bread. Run across the street to Greenblatt's and get a fresh rye bread.

EUGENE. Again? I went to the store this morning.

KATE. So you'll go again this afternoon.

EUGENE. I'm always going to the store. When I grow up, that's all I'll be trained to do, go to the store.

KATE. You don't want to go? . . . Never mind, I'll go.

EUGENE. *Don't* do that! Don't make me feel guilty. I'll go.

KATE. And get a quarter pound of butter.

EUGENE. I bought a quarter pound of butter this morning. Why don't you buy a half pound at a time?

KATE. And suppose the house burned down this afternoon? Why do I need an extra quarter pound of butter? (*She goes back into kitchen. EUGENE turns out to audience:*)

EUGENE. If my mother taught Logic in High School, this would be some weird country.

(*He runs out of the house to Greenblatt's. Our attention goes to the two girls upstairs in their room. NORA is crying. LAURIE sits on twin bed opposite her, watching.*)

LAURIE. So? . . . What are you going to do?

NORA. I don't know. Leave me alone. Don't just sit there watching me.

LAURIE. It's my room as much as yours. I don't have to leave if I don't want to.

NORA. Do you have to stare at me? Can't I have any privacy?

LAURIE. I'm staring into space. I can't help it if your body interferes. (*There is a pause.*) I bet you're worried?

NORA. How would you feel if your entire life depended on what your Uncle Jack decided? . . . Oh, God, I wish Daddy were alive.

LAURIE. He would have said, "No." He was really *strict*.

NORA. Not with me. I mean he was strict but he was fair. If he said, "No," he always gave you a good reason. He always talked things out . . . I wish I could call him somewhere now and ask him what to do. One three minute call to heaven is all I ask.

LAURIE. Ask Mom. She talks to him every night.

NORA. Who told you that?

LAURIE. She did. Every night before she goes to bed. She puts his picture on her pillow and talks to him. Then she pulls the blanket half way up the picture and goes to sleep.

NORA. She does not.

LAURIE. She does too. Last year when I had the big fever, I slept in bed with the both of them. In the middle of the night, my face fell on his picture and cut my nose.

NORA. She never told me that . . . That's weird.

LAURIE. I can't remember him much anymore. I used to remember him real good but now he disappears a little bit every day.

NORA. Oh, God, he was so handsome. Always dressed so dapper, his shoes always shined. I always thought he should have been a movie star . . . like Gary

Cooper . . . only very short. Mostly I remember his pockets.

LAURIE. His pockets?

NORA. When I was six or seven he always brought me home a little surprise. Like a Hershey or a top. He'd tell me to go get it in his coat pocket. So I'd run to the closet and put my hand in and it felt as big as a tent. I wanted to crawl in there and go to sleep. And there were all these terrific things in there, like Juicy Fruit gum or Spearment Life Savers and bits of cellophane and crumbled pieces of tobacco and movie stubs and nickels and pennies and rubber bands and paper clips and his grey suede gloves that he wore in the winter time.

LAURIE. With the stitched lines down the fingers. I remember.

NORA. Then I found his coat in Mom's closet and I put my hand in the pocket. And everything was gone. It was emptied and dry cleaned and it felt cold . . . And that's when I knew he was really dead. (*thinks a moment*) Oh God, I wish we had our own place to live. I hate being a boarder. Listen, let's make a pact . . . The first one who makes enough money promises not to spend any on herself, but saves it all to get a house for you and me and Mom. That means every penny we get from now on, we save for the house . . . We can't buy *anything*. No lipstick or magazines or nail polish or bubble gum. *Nothing* . . . Is it a pact?

LAURIE. (*thinks*) . . . What about movies?

NORA. Movies too.

LAURIE. Starting when?

NORA. Starting today. Starting right now.

LAURIE. . . . Can we start Sunday? I wanted to see *The Thin Man*.

NORA. Who's in it?

LAURIE. William Powell and Myrna Loy.

NORA. Okay. Starting Sunday . . . I'll go with you Saturday.

(*They shake hands, sealing their "pact," then both lie down in their respective beds and stare up at the ceiling, contemplating their "future home." EU-GENE returns with a paper bag containing milk and butter under his arm. He stops, pretends to be a quarterback awaiting the pass from center. The bread is his football.*)

EUGENE. . . . Sid Luckman of Columbia waits for the snap from center, the snow is coming down in a near blizzard, he gets it, he fades back, he passes . . . (*He acts all this out.*)—AND LUCKMAN'S GOT IT! LUCKMAN CATCHES HIS OWN PASS! HE'S ON THE 50, THE 40, THE 30, THE 20 . . . IT'S A TOUCHDOWN! Columbia wins! They defeat the mighty Crimson of Harvard, 13-12. Listen to that crowd! (*He roars like a crowd . . . KATE comes out of the kitchen. She yells out.*)

KATE. EUGENE! STOP THAT YELLING! I HAVE A CAKE IN THE OVEN! (*She goes back into kitchen.*)

(*STANLEY JEROME appears. STAN is eighteen and a half. He wears slacks, a shirt and tie, a zip-up jacket and a cap.*)

STAN. (*half whisper*) Hey! Eugie!

EUGENE. Hi, Stan! (*to audience*) My brother, Stan. He's okay. You'll like him. (*to STAN*) What are you doing home so early?

STAN. (*looks around, lowers his voice*) Is Pop home yet?

EUGENE. No . . . Did you ask about the tickets?

STAN. What tickets?

EUGENE. For the Yankee game. You said your boss knew this guy who could get passes. You didn't ask him?

STAN. Me and my boss had other things to talk about. (*He sits on steps, his head down, almost in tears.*) I'm in trouble, Eug. I mean really big trouble.

EUGENE. (*to audience*) This really shocked me. Because Stan is the kind of guy who could talk himself out of *any* kind of trouble. (*to STAN*) What kind of trouble?

STAN. . . . I got fired today!

EUGENE. (*shocked*) Fired? . . . You mean for good?

STAN. You don't get fired temporarily. It's permanent. It's a lifetime firing.

EUGENE. Why? What happened?

STAN. It was on account of Andrew. The colored guy who sweeps up. Well, he was cleaning the floor in the stock room and he lays his broom against the table to put some junk in the trash can and the broom slips, knocks a can of linseed oil over the table and ruins three brand new hats right out of the box. Nine dollar Stetsons. It wasn't his fault. He didn't put the linseed oil there, right?

EUGENE. Right.

STAN. So Mr. Stroheim sees the oily hats and he gets crazy. He says to Andrew the hats are going to have to come out of his salary. Twenty-seven dollars. So Andrew starts to cry.

EUGENE. He cried?

STAN. Forty-two years old, he's bawling all over the

stock room. I mean, the man hasn't got too much furniture upstairs anyway, but he's real sweet. He brings me coffee, always laughing, telling me jokes. I never understand them but I laugh anyway, make him feel good, you know?

EUGENE. Yeah?

STAN. Anyway, I said to Mr. Stroheim I didn't think that was fair. It wasn't Andrew's fault.

EUGENE. (*astounded*) You said that to him?

STAN. Sure, why not? So Mr. Stroheim says, "You wanna pay for the hats, big mouth?" So I said, "No. I don't want to pay for the hats." So he says, "Then mind your own business, big mouth."

EUGENE. Holy mackerel.

STAN. So Mr. Stroheim looks at me like machine gun bullets are coming out of his eyes. And then he calmly sends Andrew over to the factory to pick up three new hats. Which is usually my job. So guess what Mr. Stroheim tells *me* to do?

EUGENE. What?

STAN. He tells me to sweep up. He says, for this week I'm the cleaning man.

EUGENE. I can't believe it.

STAN. Everybody is watching me now, waiting to see what I'm going to do. (*EUGENE nods in agreement.*) . . . Even Andrew stopped crying and watched. I felt the dignity of everyone who worked in that store was in my hands . . . so I grit my teeth, and I pick up the broom, and there's this big pile of dirt right in the middle of the floor . . .

EUGENE. Yeah?

STAN. . . . And I sweep it all over Mr. Stroheim's shoes. Andrew had just finished shining them this morning, if you want to talk about irony.

EUGENE. I'm dying. I'm actually dying.

STAN. (*enjoying himself*) You could see everyone in the place is about to bust a gut. Mrs. Mulcahy, the bookkeeper, can hardly keep her false teeth in her mouth. Andrew's eyes are hanging five inches out of their sockets.

EUGENE. This is the greatest story in the history of the world.

STAN. So Mr. Stroehim grabs me and pulls me into his back office, closes the door and pulls down the shades. He gives me this whole story how he was brought up in Germany to respect his superiors. That if he ever—(*in accent*) "did soch a ting like you do, dey would beat me in der cup until dey carried me avay dead."

EUGENE. That's perfect. You got him down perfect.

STAN. And I say, "Yeah. But we're not in Germany, old buddy."

EUGENE. You said that to him?

STAN. No. To myself. I didn't want to go too far.

EUGENE. I was wondering.

STAN. Anyway, he says he's always liked me and always thought I was a good boy and that he was going to give me one more chance. He wants a letter of apology. And that if the letter of apology isn't on his desk by nine o'clock tomorrow morning, I can consider myself fired.

EUGENE. . . . I would have had a heart attack . . . What did you say?

STAN. I said I was not going to apologize if Andrew still had to pay for the hats . . . He said that was between him and Andrew . . . and that he expected the letter from me in the morning . . . I said good night, walked out of his office, got my hat and went home . . . ten minutes early.

EUGENE. I'm sweating. I swear to God, I'm sweating all over.

STAN. . . . I don't know why I did it. But I got so mad. It just wasn't fair. I mean, if you give in when you're eighteen and a half, you'll give in for the rest of your life, don't you think?

EUGENE. I suppose so . . . So what's the decision? Are you going to write the letter?

STAN. (*thinks . . .*) . . . No!

EUGENE. Positively?

STAN. Positively. Except I'll have to discuss it with Pop. I know we need the money. But he told me once you always have to do what you think is right in this world and stand up for your principles.

EUGENE. And what if he says he thinks you're wrong? That you should write the letter.

STAN. He won't. He's gonna leave it up to me, I know it.

EUGENE. But what if he says, "Write the letter"?

STAN. Well . . . that's something we won't know until after dinner, will we? . . . (*He crosses into the house.*)

EUGENE. (*looks after him, then turns out to audience*) . . . All in all, it was shaping up to be one heck of a dinner. I'll say this though . . . I always had this two way thing about my brother. Either I worshipped the ground he walked on . . . or I hated him so much I wanted to kill him . . . I guess you know how I feel about him today. (*He walks into the house as KATE comes out of the kitchen carrying water pitcher for the table. STAN has stopped to look at the small pile of mail.*)

KATE. (*to EUGENE*) All day it takes to bring home bread? Give Aunt Blanche the butter, she's waiting for it.

EUGENE. I was home a half hour ago. I was talking to Stan. (*He goes into kitchen.*)

STAN. (*looking at letter*) Hey, I got a letter from Rosalyn Weiner. Remember her? She moved to Manhattan. They live up on Central Park West.

KATE. Why not? Her father's a gangster, her mother is worse. I don't get a kiss "Hello"?

STAN. Nope. I was going to save it up and give you a giant one for Christmas.

KATE. We don't have Christmas. I'll take it now, thank you. (*He puts his arms around her and kisses her warmly, then embraces her.*) A hug too? When do I ever get a hug from you? You must have done something wrong.

STAN. You're too smart for me, Mom. I robbed a barber shop today.

KATE. Is that why you look so tired? You don't get enough sleep. Running around all night with your two hundred girl friends.

STAN. A hundred and thirty. That's all I have, a hundred and thirty.

KATE. How do you get any work done?

STAN. I get it done.

KATE. And your boss doesn't say anything to you? About being tired?

STAN. About being tired? No. He doesn't. (*He starts towards stairs.*)

KATE. Did you ask him about Thursday?

STAN. What?

KATE. You were going to ask him about getting paid this Thursday so I can pay Greenblatt's on Friday. Saturday is a holiday.

STAN. Oh. No. I forgot . . . I'll ask him tomorrow.

KATE. If it's a problem, don't ask him. Greenblatt can wait. Your boss is more important.

STAN. That's not true, Mom. My boss isn't any more important than Mr. Greenblatt.

(*He goes upstairs with his letter and on up to his room, where he lies down, tries to read his letter, then puts it down and stares up at the ceiling wondering about his predicament. EUGENE bursts out of the kitchen and practically staggers out of the house. He sits on the steps, his head down, looking very disconsolate. He addresses the audience.*)

EUGENE. Oh, God! . . . As if things weren't bad enough . . . And now this! . . . The ultimate tragedy . . . Liver and cabbage for dinner! . . . A Jewish mediaeval torture! . . . My friend, Marty Gregorio, an A student in Science, told me that cooked cabbage can be smelled farther than sound travelling for seven minutes . . . If these memoirs are never finished, you'll know it's because I gagged to death one night in the middle of supper.

(*We suddenly hear a crash of broken dishes in the kitchen. EUGENE turns towards the sound, then to the audience.*)

EUGENE. (*continued*) You're all witnesses. I was sitting here, right? But I'll get blamed for that anyway.

(*The kitchen door opens and KATE comes out helping BLANCHE who is wheezing and gasping quite badly. She can't catch her breath.*)

BLANCHE. I'm alright. Just let me sit a minute.
KATE. Didn't I tell you to get out of that hot kitchen?

I can't breathe in there and *I* don't have asthma. (*She calls out.*) NORA! LAURIE! Come help your mother!! (*NORA and LAURIE jump up from their beds.*)

BLANCHE. I'm sick about the plates. I'll replace them. Don't worry about the plates.

KATE. Plates I can always get. I only have one sister. (*The GIRLS have come down the stairs.*)

NORA. What happened?

BLANCHE. I'm alright. Don't run, Laurie.

KATE. It's another asthma attack. It's the second one this week. Nora, maybe you'd better get the doctor.

BLANCHE. I don't need doctors . . .

KATE. This is no climate for you, near the beach. What you need is someplace dry.

LAURIE. Like Arizona, Momma.

NORA. Should I get the doctor?

BLANCHE. No. No doctors. It's better. It's going away.

LAURIE. I can still hear the whistle.

NORA. Will you shut up!

BLANCHE. (*to NORA*) Help Aunt Kate in the kitchen, Nora. I broke her good plates.

KATE. Never mind. Eugene will do it. You go up and get your mother's medicine . . . Laurie, you sit there quiet and watch your mother. You look pale as a ghost. Eugene!

EUGENE & KATE. Come in here and help me!

JACK. (*offstage*) Hello, Mrs. Kresky, how are you?

EUGENE. (*gets up, looks off down the street*) In a minute, Ma. Pop's home! (*LAURIE sits next to her mother. To audience:*) I would now like to introduce my father a read hard worker. He was born at the age of 42 . . . Hi, Pop! How you doin', Pop?

(*JACOB "JACK" JEROME appears, a man about 40,
who could pass for older. He wears a wrinkled suit,
brown felt hat and black shoes. The* Brooklyn Eagle
*sticks up out of his side coat pocket. He carries two
large and very heavy cardboard boxes, tied around
with hemp cord. He appears to be very tired.*)

JACK. How am I doin'?

EUGENE. Let me carry these for you, Pop. (*He
reaches for one of the boxes.*)

JACK. They're too heavy, you'll hurt yourself.

EUGENE. No. I can do it easy. (*He takes one of the
boxes, tries to lift it. It weighs a ton.*) Ugh! . . . I just
have to get a good grip. (*JACK stops and sits. He wipes
his forehead with handkerchief and holds his chest.*)

JACK. I want to sit a few minutes.

EUGENE. Are you okay, Pop?

JACK. I'm resting, that's all . . . Get me a glass of cold
water.

EUGENE. I'll be out for the other box in a minute,
Pop. (*He struggles with the first box towards the house.
To audience:*) . . . I don't know how he does it. King
Kong couldn't lift these . . . You know what's in here?
Noise makers and party favors. Pop sells them to
nightclubs and hotels after he gets through every day
with his regular work, which is cutting material for
ladies' raincoats.

JACK. Did you do your homework today?

EUGENE. Not all of it. Mom sent me to the store 15
times. Amos and Andy is on tonight.

JACK. Do your homework then we'll discuss Amos
and Andy.

(*EUGENE continues into the house as NORA comes down the stairs with her mother's medicine.*)

NORA. Here's your medicine, Mom. Laurie, go get some water.

BLANCHE. Laurie shouldn't be running.

EUGENE. (*the hero*) I'll get it, Nora.

NORA. You sure you don't mind?

EUGENE. No. No trouble at all. (*to audience*) Two and a half seconds, that's all I ask. (*He goes into the kitchen.*)

NORA. (*to BLANCHE*) When are you going to speak to Uncle Jack, Mom?

BLANCHE. When I speak to him, that's when I'll speak to him.

NORA. Tonight? I have to know tonight.

BLANCHE. I'll see . . . If he's not too tired, I'll talk to him tonight. (*KATE comes out of the kitchen.*)

KATE. Jack's home. We'll eat in ten minutes. Nora, darling, go get Stanley . . . How's your mother, Laurie?

LAURIE. Much better. The whistling's stopped.

(*KATE crosses to the front door and goes out. JACK is sitting on the stoop, wiping his neck. NORA goes upstairs.*)

KATE. What's wrong? Eugene said you were holding your chest.

JACK. I wasn't holding my chest.

KATE. You have to carry that box every day? Back and forth to the city. You don't work hard enough, Jack?

JACK. You want the box, it's yours. Keep it. I don't need it anymore.

KATE. What do you mean?

JACK. Del Mars Party Favors went out of business. They closed him out. The man is bankrupt.

KATE. Oh, my God!

JACK. He never even warned me it was coming.

KATE. You told me he lived up on Riverside Drive. With a view of the river. A three hundred dollar a month apartment he had. A man like that.

JACK. Who are the ones you think go bankrupt? You live in a cold water flat on Delancey Street, bankruptcy is the one thing God spares you.

KATE. Alright . . . You can always find good in something. You don't have to lug that box anymore. You don't have to get up at five-thirty in the morning. We can all eat dinner at a decent hour. You still have your job with Jacobson, we won't starve.

JACK. I can't make ends meet with what I make at Jacobson's. Not with seven people to feed.

KATE. (*looks back towards the house*) They'll hear you. We'll talk later.

JACK. I can't get by without that extra twenty-five dollars a week. I can't pay rent and insurance and food and clothing for seven people. Christmas and New Year's alone I made a hundred and fifty dollars.

KATE. (*nervous about anyone hearing*) Stop it, Jack. You'll only get yourself sick.

JACK. He didn't even pay me for the week, the bastard. Five salesman are laid off and he's going to a Broadway show tonight. I stuffed every hat and noise maker I could carry in that box and walked out of there. At his funeral I'll put on a pointy hat and blow a horn, the bastard!

KATE. Don't talk like that. Something'll come up. You'll go to temple this weekend. You'll pray all day Saturday.

JACK. (*smiles ironically*) There's men in that temple

who've been praying for forty years. You know how
many prayers have to get answered before my turn
comes up?

KATE. (*She rubs his back where it pains him.*) Your
turn'll come up. God has time for everybody. (*EU-
GENE has come out of the kitchen with two glasses
of water. He crosses to BLANCHE.*)

EUGENE. Here's your water, Aunt Blanche.

BLANCHE. Thank you, darling.

EUGENE. Where's Nora?

LAURIE. She went up to call Stanley for dinner.

EUGENE. Hey, Laurie. You want to take a walk on the
beach tonight?

LAURIE. I have homework. What do you want to walk
with me for?

EUGENE. You, me and Nora. I just felt like taking a
walk.

LAURIE. I think Nora has a date with Larry Clurman.

EUGENE. *Larry Clurman??* . . . She likes Larry Clurman?

LAURIE. I don't know. Ask her yourself.

EUGENE. Larry Clurman is my father's age.

LAURIE. He's twenty.

EUGENE. Same thing . . . You think he's good-
looking?

LAURIE. I don't think *anybody's* good-looking.

EUGENE. Larry Clurman? He doesn't even have a
chin. His tie comes all the way up to his teeth.

KATE. (*calls out*) Eugene! Where's your father's
water?

EUGENE. I'm coming! I'm coming. (*As he crosses to
front door, he turns to the audience.*) Now I've got
Larry Clurman to contend with. (*He comes out.*) Here's
your water, Pop. I put ice in it. (*He hands father glass
of water. He drinks it all.*)

KATE. Don't drink so fast.

EUGENE. Do you have time to look at my sneakers, Pop?

KATE. What does he want to look at your sneakers for?

EUGENE. They have no soles. They're hanging on by a tiny piece of rubber. I have to clench my toes when I run out for a fly ball.

JACK. I bought you new sneakers last month.

EUGENE. Last year, Pa. Not last month. I can only wear them two hours a day because my toes can't grow in them.

KATE. This is no time to talk to your father about sneakers. He's got enough on his mind. Turn the light down on the liver. (*EUGENE goes into the house and into the kitchen. To JACK:*) We'll talk about this tonight. You'll eat a nice dinner, relax and when everybody's asleep, we'll figure things out calmly. I don't like it when you get upset.

BLANCHE. I'm feeling better. Come, dear, help me with dinner. (*She goes into kitchen.*)

JACK. (*looks at house*) You think she'll ever get married?

KATE. Blanche?

JACK. She's not unattractive. I see men look at her on the beach. What does she want to waste her life in this house for?

KATE. She's raising two children.

JACK. Why doesn't she ever go out? If she wants to meet people, I know plenty of single men.

KATE. Blanche isn't the type to get married.

JACK. She was married once, wasn't she? Those are the type that get married.

KATE. Dave was different. She's not interested in other men.

JACK. What about that Murphy fellow across the street? He's plenty interested, believe me.

KATE. That drunk! The man can't find his way into the house at night. He slept in the doorway once. In the rain. He was there when I went out to get the milk.

JACK. He's got a good paying job, lives alone with his mother. So he takes a drink on a Saturday night. Maybe what he needs is a good woman.

KATE. Not my sister. Let him meet someone lying in the next doorway. I don't want to discuss this anymore.

(*She goes into the house and into the kitchen. The father sighs, gets up slowly and follows her in. Our attention goes to STANLEY on his bed still reading the letter from Rosalyn Weiner. He suddenly sits up. NORA knocks on his door.*)

STAN. Come in. (*NORA comes in.*)

NORA. Are you busy? I wanted to talk to you.

STAN. That's funny, because I wanted to talk to *you*.

NORA. About what?

STAN. I need a favor. Real bad. You're the only one who can help me.

NORA. What is it?

STAN. Well, when Pop comes home tired, he doesn't usually pay too much attention to me and Eugene. He's different with you. He's always interested in what you have to say.

NORA. Really? I hope so.

STAN. Oh, sure. You never noticed that?

NORA. Not really. What's the favor?

STAN. This may sound dumb, but at dinner, do you think you could steer the conversation in a certain direction?

NORA. What direction?

STAN. Well, something like "how much you admire people who stand up for their principles."

NORA. *What* people?

STAN. *Any* people. Principles is the important word. If you could work it in three or four times, I'd be very grateful.

NORA. Three or four times??

STAN. It'll be easy. I'll mention someone like Abraham Lincoln and you look up and say, "Now there's a man who really stood up for his principles."

NORA. I have my *own* things to bring up at dinner. I don't want to get into a discussion about Abraham Lincoln.

STAN. Not his whole life. Just his principles.

NORA. Why would I do such a stupid thing?

STAN. . . . Because as of tomorrow I'm unemployed . . . unless someone besides me mentions "sticking up for your principles."

NORA. What happened? Did you get fired?

STAN. I will be unless I write Kaiser Wilhelm a letter of apology. It's really up to my old man. I've decided to do whatever he tells me . . .

NORA. When are you going to ask him?

STAN. Tonight. Right after dinner.

NORA. *Tonight?* Does it have to be tonight?

STAN. That's the deadline. I have to give my answer to Mr. Stroheim in the morning. Why?

NORA. Couldn't you ask your father in the morning?

STAN. He gets up at five-thirty. My mother has to line up his shoes at night because he can't make decisions at five-thirty. (*She is about to break into tears.*) What's wrong, Nora?

NORA. (*angrily*) I don't know what *you* have to complain about. At least your father is alive and around the house to make decisions. You don't know when you're well off, Stanley. Sometimes you make me sick!

(*She runs out of the room, slamming the door behind her. STANLEY sits there looking bewildered. EUGENE crosses into the dining room and is the first one seated, facing the audience. He looks at them and speaks.*)

EUGENE. Chapter Seven. "The Infamous Dinner"! (*The others drift into the dining room, taking their seats. BLANCHE and KATE bring most of the dishes, passing them around. They are all seated as EUGENE continues his narrative.*) . . . It started out like a murder mystery in Blenheim Castle. No one said a word but everyone looked suspicious . . . It was so quiet, you could hear Laurie's soup going down her esophagus. (*They sit quietly, eating.*) Everyone had one eye on their plate and the other eye on Pop. Except me. I sat opposite Nora. I kept dropping my napkin a lot so I could bend down to get a good look at those virginal creamy-white legs. She was really deep in thought because she left herself unguarded a few times and I got to see half way up her thighs that led to the Golden Palace of the Himalayas.

KATE. Eugene! Keep your napkin on your lap and stop daydreaming.

EUGENE. (*to audience*) Stanley knew what I was doing because he's the one who taught it to me. But he was busy with his own problems like everyone else. You could hear the clock ticking in the kitchen. The tension in the air was so thick, you could cut it with a knife. Which is more than I could say for the liver. (*He tries to cut his liver.*)

JACK. Ketchup . . . Mustard . . . Pickles . . .

EUGENE. . . . I'm through. I'll help with the dessert.

KATE. Finish your liver.

EUGENE. I finished. Do you see liver on my plate?

KATE. You buried it under the mashed potatoes. I know your tricks. Look how Laurie ate hers.

EUGENE. (*to audience*) I had a major problem. One more bite and I would have thrown up on the table. That's a sight Nora would have remembered forever. A diversion was my only escape from humiliation. (*to STANLEY*) So how's things down at Stroheim's, Stanley? (*STANLEY is drinking water, slams down glass, splashing it. He glares at EUGENE. To audience:*) I felt bad about that, but for the moment, attention had shifted away from my liver.

JACK. (*to STANLEY*) How long have you been working there now?

STAN. Where?

JACK. At Stroheim's.

STAN. At Stroheim's? Let me see . . . Part-time a year and a half before I graduated high school. And a year since then.

JACK. So what's that?

STAN. Two and a half years, counting part-time.

JACK. And he likes you?

STAN. Who?

JACK. (*impatiently*) Mr. Stroheim.

STAN. Yeah. Usually he likes me. Sometimes I'm not sure.

JACK. You come in on time?

STAN. Yeah.

JACK. You do your work?

STAN. Yeah.

JACK. You get along with the other people?

STAN. Yeah.

JACK. So why shouldn't he like you? How much are you making now?

STAN. Seventeen dollars a week.

JACK. It's time you moved up. Tomorrow you go in and ask him for a raise.

STAN. A RAISE???

JACK. If you don't speak up, people take advantage of you. Tomorrow morning you go into his office, you're polite, you're respectful, but you're firm. You tell him you think you're worth another five dollars a week.

STAN. *FIVE DOLLARS????*

JACK. He'll offer you a dollar and a quarter, you settle for two-fifty. I know how these things work. You're a high school graduate, he's lucky he's got you.

STAN. I don't think this is the time to ask him for a raise, Pop. I think his wife is very sick.

JACK. You're afraid to ask him? You want me to take you by the hand and walk into his office and say, "My little boy wants a raise"?

STAN. I'm not afraid.

KATE. Your father wouldn't ask you if he didn't think it was the right thing. Believe me, Stanley, now is the time to ask for it.

EUGENE. (*choking*) Ma, I think I have a bone in my throat.

KATE. There are no bones in liver. (*He runs into kitchen.*)

LAURIE. So what's new at dancing school, Nora?

NORA. (*glares at her*) *Nothing* is new. Mind your own business.

LAURIE. I'm just trying to introduce the subject.

NORA. I don't need your help. Will you tell her to be quiet, Mother.

BLANCHE. (*to NORA*) Laurie, you may be excused if you're finished.

JACK. What happened at dancing school?

BLANCHE. Nora received a very nice compliment from her teacher. She said Nora had professional potential.

LAURIE. He didn't say "potential." "Potential" is the future. Mr. Beckman is interested in Nora's "immediate present."

JACK. (*still eating*) Isn't that something! Mr. Beckman is your teacher?

NORA. No. He's one of the most widely known and respected producers on Broadway.

JACK. Broadway? Imagine that? That's wonderful. And how are you doing in school otherwise?

NORA. (*looks at her mother*) I'm doing fine.

BLANCHE. She's doing very well.

LAURIE. I wish *I* was as smart as she is.

EUGENE. Isn't that the same Mr. Beckman who's producing the great Broadway extravaganza, *Abracadabra?* I hear if a girl gets hired for the chorus of a show like that, not only is her career practically guaranteed, but the experience she gains is equal to a four year college education.

KATE. Eugene, that's enough.

JACK. Only a four year college education is equal to a four year college education.

STAN. I don't think Abraham Lincoln went to college. (*NORA goes into kitchen.*)

JACK. What about you, Laurie? You're feeling alright?

LAURIE. Yes, Uncle Jack.

JACK. You getting plenty of fresh air? (*NORA returns.*)

LAURIE. As much as I can hold in my lungs. Nora, did you tell Uncle Jack about the big tank that's filled with water.

BLANCHE. Girls, why don't we just let Uncle Jack eat

his dinner? If we have something to discuss, we can discuss it later?

JACK. Somebody has something to discuss? If there's a problem, this is the time to bring it up. This is the family hour.

EUGENE. What a great idea for a radio show. The family hour. Every Wednesday night you hear a different family eating dinner discussing their problems of the week. And you get to hear different recipes. (*as announcer*) WEAF presents dinner at Brighton Beach starring the Jacob Jerome Family and featuring tonight's speciality liver and cabbage, brought to you by Ex-lax, the mild laxative.

KATE. The whole country's going to hear about a fifteen year old boy gagging on liver?

JACK. Nothing to discuss? Nobody has any problems? Otherwise I want to turn on the news.

STAN. Well, as a matter of fact . . .

JACK. What?

STAN. Nothing.

EUGENE. I'll help with the dishes.

KATE. You sit there and finish your liver.

EUGENE. I can't swallow it. It won't go down. Remember the lima bean catastrophe last month? Does anybody want to see a repeat of that disgusting episode?

JACK. Why does he always talk like it's a Sherlock Holmes story?

STAN. He thinks he's a writer.

EUGENE. And what do you think *you* are?

KATE. Eat half of it.

EUGENE. Which half? They're both terrible.

KATE. A quarter of it. Two bites.

EUGENE. *One* bite.

KATE. *Two* bites.

EUGENE. I know you. If I eat one bite, you'll make me eat another bite . . . I'll take it to my room. I'll eat it tonight. I need time to chew it.

JACK. These are not times to waste food. If you didn't want it, Eugene, you shouldn't have taken it.

EUGENE. I didn't take it. They gave it to me. It comes attached to the plate.

NORA. If it's so important to everybody, I'll eat your liver, Eugene. (*They all look at her.*)

EUGENE. You *will?*

NORA. It seems to be the only thing this family is worried about. Give me your liver so we can get on with more important things in our lives.

JACK. Nora's right. Take the liver away. If nobody likes it, why do you make it?

KATE. (*angrily*) Because we can't afford a roast beef for seven people. (*She heads for the kitchen.*)

EUGENE. (*to audience*) I suddenly felt vulgar and cheap.

JACK. Stanley, turn on the news.

BLANCHE. Laurie, get off your feet. You look tired to me.

STAN. Can I talk to you a minute, Pop? It's something really important.

JACK. More important than what's going on in Europe? (*He turns radio on.*)

STAN. It's not more important. It's just coming up sooner.

JACK. (*fiddles with stations*) Hitler's already moved into Austria. In a couple of months the whole world will be in it . . . What's the matter with this radio?

KATE. (*comes out of kitchen*) Someone's been fooling around with it. Haven't they, Eugene?

EUGENE. Why Eugene? Pop had the news on last night.

KATE. You weren't listening to the ball game this afternoon? (*The radio is barely audible.*)

JACK. He's talking about Poland . . . Dammit! I don't want anyone touching this radio anymore, you understand?

EUGENE. (*to audience*) Guess who's gonna get blamed for the war in Europe?

KATE. Eugene! Bring in the knives and forks. (*He does. JACK turns radio off.*)

STAN. You really think there'll be war, Pop? I mean America, too?

JACK. We're already in it. Not us maybe. But friends, relatives. If you're Jewish, you've got a cousin suffering *somewhere* in the world.

KATE. (*wiping table*) Ida Kazinsky's family got out of Poland last month. The stories she tells about what's going on there, you don't even want to hear.

STAN. How many relatives do we have in Europe?

KATE. Enough. Uncles, cousins. I have a great-aunt. Your father has nephews.

JACK. I have a cousin, Sholem, in Poland. His whole family.

BLANCHE. Dave had relatives in Warsaw. That's where his mother was born.

STAN. What if they got to America? Where would they live?

JACK. Who?

STAN. Your nephews. Mom's cousins and uncles. Would we take them in? (*JACK looks at KATE.*)

JACK. What God gives us to deal with, we deal with.

STAN. Where would we put them?

KATE. What are you worrying about things like that now for? Go upstairs and work on your speech.

STAN. What speech?

KATE. How you're going to ask Mr. Stroheim for a raise tomorrow. (*STANLEY looks apprehensively at EUGENE.*)

STAN. Can I talk to you later, Pop? After you've rested and read your paper?

EUGENE. (*has taken part of father's papers, opens it*) Lou Gehrig got two hits today. Larrupin Lou is hitting three-oh-two!

KATE. (*grabs paper away*) Is that your paper? How many times have I told you you don't read it until your father is finished?

EUGENE. I didn't break it. The print doesn't come off if I take a quick look at it.

JACK. Don't be fresh to your mother. Upstairs.

STAN. Pop?

JACK. Everybody.

STAN. I'll come down later, O.K., Pop?

EUGENE. C'mon, Stan. I have to talk to you anyway. (*They start towards stairs.*)

STAN. (*to EUGENE*) You're a pest! Did anyone ever tell you you're a pest?

EUGENE. Yeah. I have a list upstairs. You wanna add your name to it. (*He taps STANLEY on the forehead with his forefinger. It is annoying and STAN chases him up the stairs.*)

KATE. (*to JACK*) Maybe you should lie down. There's nothing in that paper that's going to cheer you up.

JACK. (*thoughtfully*) What *would* we do, Kate? Where would we put them if they got off the boat and knocked on our door? How would we feed them?

KATE. The boat didn't get here yet. I can't deal with boats that haven't landed yet.

(*NORA bursts out of the kitchen, apparently having just argued with her mother. She is followed by BLANCHE and LAURIE.*)

NORA. (*determined*) Uncle Jack! I know you're tired and you have a lot of things on your mind but the rest of my life may depend on your decision and I have to know tonight because I have to call Mr. Beckman and let him know if I can go or not.

JACK. Who's Mr. Beckman?

NORA. The Broadway producer we talked about at dinner.

LAURIE. *Abracadabra?* Remember? (*STANLEY crosses to bathroom—EUGENE crosses into bedroom.*)

BLANCHE. Laurie! Upstairs! This minute . . . Nora, not now. This isn't the time.

NORA. (*angrily*) It's *never* the time. You won't make a decision and I don't have anyone else I can talk to. Well, I'll make my own decision if no one else is interested. I'm sixteen and a half years old and I'll do what I *want* to do. (*The tears begin to flow as she runs out the front door to the yard.*)

JACK. What is this all about?

KATE. Go on out, Jack. Talk to her.

BLANCHE. I'll take care of it. Nora's right. It's my decision.

KATE. What are you going to tell her? That she can leave school? That she can throw her future away? Is that what you want to do?

BLANCHE. What if I'm wrong? What if she's got talent? What is it I'm *supposed* to say?

JACK. She can't talk to me? It's all the same family, isn't it? I'm her uncle, for God's sake.

KATE. She doesn't need an uncle tonight. She needs a father . . . Go on. She'll tell you. (*JACK looks at the both of them, then walks out the door to the front yard. NORA is sitting on the bench, tearfully.*)

BLANCHE. I never learned.

JACK. You mind if I sit with you?

BLANCHE. I wrapped my life up in Dave so much, I never learned to be their mother.

JACK. If you want to talk, we'll talk, if not, not.

KATE. We have enough mothers here. This is a family. The world doesn't survive without families . . . Laurie, do your homework. Blanche, make me some tea. You're the only one here who makes decent tea.

(*LAURIE goes up to her room. STANLEY and EUGENE are in their room. BLANCHE and KATE have gone into the kitchen. JACK is outside with NORA.*)

JACK. Listen . . . I know what it's like, Nora. Not to be heard.

NORA. You do?

JACK. I grew up in a family of four children. My father, before he died, never could remember our names. My oldest brother was "the big one," I was "the little one." My brother Sol was "the rotten one," Eddie was "the skinny one."

NORA. Who am I?

JACK. The pretty one . . . What's the problem?

(*STANLEY comes out of bathroom, crosses to window
    stage* R., *then crosses into bedroom.*)

NORA. I don't know. It doesn't seem very important
now.

JACK. I've never seen you cry over something that
wasn't important. I know I'm not your father. It's not
my place to make decisions for you. But I can offer advice. Advice is free. If it doesn't fit, you can always
return it.

NORA. . . . Can we walk down the block?

JACK. Sure. We'll take a look at the ocean. My father
always used to say, "Throw your problems out to sea
and the answers will wash back up on the shore."

NORA. Did they?

JACK. Not in Brighton Beach. Orange peels and
watermelon pits washed up. That's why it's good to take
someone who knows how to give advice.

(*She gets up and they walk off towards the beach.
    STANLEY is lying on his bed, hands under his
    head, deep in thought. EUGENE sits on his bed,
    banging a baseball into his glove.*)

STAN. Will you stop that? I'm trying to think.

EUGENE. I'm glad I don't have your problems.

STAN. How'd you like an official American League
baseball in your mouth?

EUGENE. I've got to talk to you, Stanley. I mean a
really, serious, important talk.

STAN. Everybody in this house has to have a talk with
somebody. Take a number off the wall and wait your
turn.

EUGENE. I had a dream last night. It was about this

girl. I can't tell you her name but she's gorgeous. We were really kissing hard and rubbing up against each other and I felt this tremendous buildup coming like at the end of *The Thirty-Nine Steps.* And suddenly there was an explosion. Like a dam broke and everything rushed and flowed out to sea. It was the greatest feeling I ever had in my life . . . and when I woke up, I was—I was—

STAN. All wet.

EUGENE. (*surprised*) Yeah! How'd you know?

STAN. (*unimpressed*) It was a wet dream. You had a wet dream. I have them all the time.

EUGENE. You do? You mean there's nothing wrong with you if it happens?

STAN. You never had one before?

EUGENE. Yeah, but I slept through it.

STAN. Didn't you ever try to do it by yourself?

EUGENE. What do you mean?

STAN. Didn't you ever diddle with yourself?

EUGENE. No. Never.

STAN. Baloney. I've heard you. You diddle three, four times a week.

EUGENE. You're crazy! What do you mean, diddle?

STAN. Whack off. Masturbate.

EUGENE. Will you be quiet! Laurie might hear you.

STAN. There's nothing wrong with it. Everybody does it. Especially at our age. It's natural.

EUGENE. What do you mean, everybody? You know guys who do it?

STAN. Every guy I know does it. Except Haskell Fleischman, the fat kid. He does it to the other guys.

EUGENE. I can't believe I'm having this conversation.

STAN. You can't grow up without doing it. Your voice won't change.

EUGENE. Where do you get this stuff from? Is it in a medical book or something?

STAN. It's puberty.

EUGENE. It's what?

STAN. Puberty. You never heard that word before? You don't read books?

EUGENE. Yeah. *The Citadel* by A.J. Cronin. He never mentioned puberty.

STAN. Even Pop did it.

EUGENE. Pop? *Our* pop? You know what, Stanley? I think you're full of shit.

STAN. (*sits up*) Hey! Don't you use that language. Who do you think you are? You're just a kid. Never let me hear you say that word again.

EUGENE. I don't get you. You mean it's okay for you to say "puberty" but I can't say "shit"?

STAN. Puberty is a scientific word. Shit is for those guys who hang around the beach.

EUGENE. What do you expect me to say when you tell me that Pop whacks off?

STAN. I don't mean he still does it because he's married now. But when he was a kid. Fourteen or fifteen. The whole world whacks off.

EUGENE. . . . President Roosevelt too?

STAN. Rich kids are the worst. They whack off from morning till night. In college, they sit around in their dorms drinking beer and whacking off.

EUGENE. Stanley, this is the most useful information you ever taught me . . . What about girls?

STAN. Five times as much as boys.

EUGENE. *Five* times as much? Is that an actual figure? Where do you know all this from?

STAN. You pick it up. You learn it. It's handed down from generation to generation. That's how our culture spreads.

EUGENE. Five times as much as boys? Some of them don't even say "hello" to you and they're home all night whacking off.

STAN. They're human just like we are. They have the same needs and desires.

EUGENE. Then why is it so hard to touch their boobs?

STAN. If you were a girl, would you like some guy jumping at you and grabbing your boobs?

EUGENE. If I had boobs, I would love to touch them, wouldn't you?

STAN. I've got my own problems to think about.

EUGENE. How do girls do it?

STAN. I can't explain it.

EUGENE. Please, Stanley. I'll be your slave for a month. Tell me how they do it.

STAN. I need a pencil and paper. I'll do it later.

EUGENE. (*quickly hands him his notebook and a pencil*) Do you want crayons? Maybe you should do it in color?

STAN. Hey, Eugene. I have a major problem in my life. I haven't got time to draw girls masturbating for you.

EUGENE. I'll bet Nora doesn't do it.

STAN. Boy, could I win money from you. You think she's in the bathroom seven times a day just taking showers?

EUGENE. She does it in the bathroom?

STAN. I knew two girls who used to do it in English class. I saw a girl do it during a final exam and got a ninety-eight on her paper. Is she the one you were thinking about last night?

EUGENE. No. It was somebody else. One of the beach girls.

STAN. It was Nora. I see what's going on. I knew why

you dropped your napkin twelve times at dinner tonight.

EUGENE. She drives me crazy. I think I'm in love with her.

STAN. Yeah? Well, forget it. She's your cousin.

EUGENE. What's wrong with being in love with your cousin?

STAN. Because it's against the laws of nature. If she was your step-sister, it would be dirty, but it would be okay. But you can't love your own cousin. Let me give you a piece of advice. When you're going through puberty, don't start with anyone in your own house.

EUGENE. Who made up those rules? Franklin Roosevelt married his cousin.

STAN. Maybe she was his second or third cousin. But you can't marry your first cousin. You get babies with nine heads. I wish Pop would get back. I got to talk to him tonight.

EUGENE. I still would love to see her naked. Just once. There's nothing wrong with that, is there?

STAN. No. I do it all the time.

EUGENE. *You've seen Nora naked?*

STAN. Lots of times. I fixed the lock on the bathroom door then open it pretending I didn't know anyone was in there.

EUGENE. I can't believe it. What a pig! . . . What did she look like?

STAN. All I can tell you is I was pretty miserable she was my first cousin. (*STANLEY lies back on his bed. EUGENE turns and looks out at the audience.*)

EUGENE. . . . That was the night I discovered lust and guilt were very closely related. I have to wash up.

STAN. Have a good time.

EUGENE. I don't do that.

(BLANCHE and KATE come out of the kitchen. They each have a cup of tea. They sit at dining table.)

KATE. . . . I'm sorry. I forgot it was this Tuesday. I'll change my doctor appointment.

BLANCHE. You don't have to change anything. The girls will be with me.

KATE. Have I ever missed a year going to the grave? Dave was my favorite in the whole family, you know that.

BLANCHE. You realize it'll be six years? Sometimes I forget his birthday, but the day he died I never forget.

KATE. There wasn't another one like him.

BLANCHE. Laurie asks me questions about him all the time. Was he funny? What was the funniest thing he ever said, she asked me. I couldn't remember. Isn't that awful, Kate?

KATE. Sometimes you talk like your life is over. You're still a young woman. You're still beautiful, if you'd ever stop squinting so much.

BLANCHE. I went with him for two years before we were married. What was I waiting for? That's two married years I didn't have with him.

KATE. Listen. Jack's company is having their annual affair in New York next Wednesday. At the Commodore Hotel. You should see how some of those women get dressed up. Jack wants you to come with us. He told me to ask you.

BLANCHE. Me? Who do I know in Jack's company?

KATE. You'll be with *us*. You'll meet people. Max Green'll be at our table. He's the one whose wife died last year from (*whispers*) "tuberculosis" . . . He's their number one salesman. He lives in a hotel on the Grand Concourse. He's a riot. You'll like him. Maybe you'll dancc with him. What else are you going to do here every night?

BLANCHE. I don't have a dress to wear for a thing like that.

KATE. You'll make something. Jack'll get you some material. He knows everybody in the garment district.

BLANCHE. Thank you, Kate. I appreciate it. I can't go. Maybe next year. (*She gets up.*)

KATE. Next year you won't have any eyes altogether. What are you afraid of, Blanche? Dave is dead. You're not. If God wanted the both of you, you'd by laying in the grave next to him.

BLANCHE. I've made plans for next Wednesday night.

KATE. More important than this? They have this affair once a year.

BLANCHE. I'm having dinner with someone.

KATE. You're having dinner? With a man? That's wonderful. Why didn't you tell me?

BLANCHE. With Mr. Murphy. (*This stops KATE right in her tracks.*)

KATE. Who's Mr. Murphy? . . . Oh, my God! I don't understand you. You're going to dinner with that man? Do you know where he'll take you? To a saloon. To a Bar and Grill, that's where he'll take you.

BLANCHE. We're going to Chardov's, the Hungarian Restaurant. You never even met the man, why do you dislike him so much?

KATE. I don't have to meet that kind. I just have to smell his breath when he opens the window. What do you think a man like that is looking for? I grew up with that kind on Avenue A. How many times have Stanley and Gene come home from school black and blue from the beatings they took from those Irish hooligans? What have you got to talk to with a man like that?

BLANCHE. Is that why you don't like him? Because he's Irish? When have the Jews and the Irish ever fought a war? You know who George Bernard Shaw is?

KATE. I don't care who he is.

BLANCHE. One of the greatest Irish writers in the world? What would you say if *he* took me to Chardov's next Wednesday?

KATE. Is Mr. Murphy a writer? Tell him to bring me some of his books, I'll be glad to read them.

BLANCHE. Kate, when are you going to give up being an older sister?

KATE. I've heard stories about him. With women. They like their women, you know. Well, if that's what you want, it's your business.

EUGENE. (*to audience*) I decided to go downstairs and quiet my passion with oatmeal cookies.

BLANCHE. We took a walk along the beach last Thursday. He hardly said a word. He's very shy. Very quiet. He told me where his parents come from in Ireland. Their life wasn't any easier than Mamma and Pappa's in Russia.

KATE. *Nobody* had it like they had it in Russia.

BLANCHE. He holds down a decent job in a printers' office and he didn't smell of liquor and he behaved like a perfect gentleman. (*EUGENE comes down the stairs. He had been listening.*)

KATE. (*without turning*) No cookies for you. Not until you eat that liver.

EUGENE. You're still saving it? You mean it's going to be in the ice box until I grow up?

KATE. No cookies, you hear me?

EUGENE. I just want a glass of water.

KATE. You have water in your bathroom.

EUGENE. There's toothpaste in the glass. It makes me nauseous. (*He goes into the kitchen.*)

KATE. (*to BLANCHE*) Listen, there's no point discussing this. I'm going to bed. Do what you want.

BLANCHE. Kate! . . . I don't want to do anything that's going to make you unhappy. Or Jack. I owe too much to you. I can't live off you the rest of my life. Every decent job I've tried to get, they turn me down because of my eyes. The thought of marrying Frank Murphy hasn't even occured to me. Maybe not even to him. But I don't think one dinner at Chardov's is the end of the world.

KATE. I just don't want to see you get hurt. I never mean you harm. I can take anything except when someone in the family is mad at me.

BLANCHE. (*crosses and embraces her*) I could never be mad at you, Kate. That I promise you to my dying day.

KATE. Go on. Have dinner with Frank Murphy. If Poppa ever heard me say those words, he'd get up from the cemetery and stand in front of our house with a big stick. (*BLANCHE kisses her again.*)

BLANCHE. I told him to pick me up here. Is that alright?

KATE. *Here? In my* house?

BLANCHE. For two minutes. I wanted you to meet him. At least see what he's like.

KATE. Tell his mother to wash her windows, maybe I'd know what he's like.

(*We see NORA hurriedly cross the front yard and open the front door. She looks upset. NORA crosses to her mother, determined.*)

NORA. Can I see Mr. Beckman tomorrow? Yes or no? (*JACK crosses the front yard.*)

BLANCHE. Did you talk to Uncle Jack?

NORA. I talked to Uncle Jack. I want an answer from *you,* Mother. Yes or no? (*JACK enters the house.*)

BLANCHE. What did he say?

NORA. It doesn't matter what he said. It's your decision or mine. Who's going to make it, Mother?

JACK. I said if I were her father, I'd tell her to finish high school. If she's got talent, there'll be plenty of other shows. I never got past the eighth grade and that's why I spend half my life on the subway and the other half trying to make a few extra dollars to keep this family from being out on the street.

NORA. (*to BLANCHE*) I don't want this just for myself, Momma. But for you and for Laurie. In a few years we could have a house of our own, instead of all being cooped up here like animals. We could pay Uncle Jack for what he's given us all these years. I'm asking for a way out, Momma. Don't shut me in. Don't shut me in for the rest of my life. (*They all turn and look at BLANCHE.*)

BLANCHE. You promised you'd do what Uncle Jack said.

NORA. He doesn't make decisions. He offers advice. I want a decision, Momma. From you . . . Please!

BLANCHE. . . . You finish high school. You tell Mr. Beckman you're too young. You tell him your mother said, "No" . . . That's my decision.

NORA. (*looks at her, frustrated*) . . . I see. (*to JACK*) Thank you very much, Uncle Jack, for your advice. (*to BLANCHE*) I'll let you know in the morning what *my* decision is. (*She rushes upstairs to her room. BLANCHE starts to go after her.*)

KATE. Let her go, Blanche. You'll only make it worse.

BLANCHE. It seems no matter *what* I do, I only make it worse. (*She turns, starts up stairs. NORA has slammed the door of her room. STANLEY hears it and opens his door and starts down.*)

JACK. (*to KATE*) What could I tell her? What could I say?

KATE. (*shrugs*) You inherit a family, you inherit their problems.

EUGENE. (*comes out of kitchen*) Well, goodnight.

KATE. Put the cookie on the table.

EUGENE. What cookie?

KATE. The oatmeal cookie in your pocket. Put it on the table.

EUGENE. You can smell an oatmeal cookie from ten feet away?

KATE. I heard the jar moving in the kitchen. Suddenly everybody's doing what they want in this house. Your father's upset, Aunt Blanche is upset, *put the cookie on that table!* (*EUGENE puts the cookie on the table and starts up the stairs to his room. He passes STANLEY.*)

STAN. (*to EUGENE*) I heard a lot of yelling. What happened?

EUGENE. I don't know, but it's my fault. (*He goes on up and into the bathroom. NORA is on her bed, crying. LAURIE sits on her bed and watches her.*)

LAURIE. What are you going to do? (*NORA shakes her head, indicating she doesn't know.*) Do you want *me* to speak to Mom? I could tell her I was getting flutters in my heart again.

NORA. (*turns, angrily*) Don't you ever say that! Don't you pretend to be sick to get favors from anyone.

LAURIE. I'm not pretending. They're just not *big* flutters.

(*STANLEY has been sitting at the top of the stairs try-*

*ing to work up courage to talk to his father. JACK
is sitting in the living room, disconsolate. KATE is
puffing up pillows.)*

JACK. Stop puffing up pillows. The house could be
burning down and you'd run back in to puff the pillows.

KATE. Let's go to bed. You're tired.

JACK. When does it get easier, Kate? When does our
life get easier?

KATE. At night. When you get seven good hours of
sleep. That's the easiest it ever gets. (*NORA has put on
her robe, left her room and opens the bathroom door.
We hear a scream from EUGENE.*)

EUGENE. *CLOSE THE DOOR!!!*

NORA. Oh. I'm sorry. I didn't know anyone was in
there. (*She rushes out, back to her room. STANLEY
moves into the living room.*)

STAN. Dad? Do you think I could talk to you now?
It'll just take five minutes.

KATE. He's tired, Stanley. He's practically asleep.

STAN. Two minutes. I'll tell it as fast as I can.

JACK. Go on, Kate. Go to bed. The boy wants to tell
me something.

KATE. Turn out the lights when you're through. (*She
kisses JACK's head.*) Don't worry about things. We've
always made them work out. (*She leaves the room just
as EUGENE darts out of the bathroom, rushes into his
own room and slams the door.*)

EUGENE. She saw me on the crapper! Nora saw me on
the crapper! (*He falls on his bed.*) I might as well be
dead.

STAN. I have a problem, Pop.

JACK. If you didn't, you wouldn't live in this house.

STAN. It must be tough being a father. Everybody

comes to you with their problems. You have to have all the answers. I don't know if *I* could handle it.

JACK. Stop trying to win me over. Just tell me the problem.

STAN. I got fired today!

JACK. *WHAT???*

STAN. Don't get excited! Don't get crazy! Let me explain what happened.

JACK. What did you do? You came in late? You were fresh to somebody? Were you fresh to sombody?

STAN. I'm not fired yet. I can still get my job back. I just need you to help me make a decision.

JACK. Take the job back. I don't care what it is. This is *not* the time for anybody to be out of work in this family.

STAN. When I was twelve years old you gave me a talk about principles. Remember?

JACK. All night you waited to tell me this news?

STAN. This is about principles, Pop.

JACK. How long were you going to go without telling me?

STAN. Will you at least hear my principles?

JACK. Alright, I'll hear your principles. Then you'll hear mine.

STAN. Just sit back and let me tell you what happened. Okay? Well it was on account of Andrew the colored guy who sweeps up.

(*JACK sits back and listens. STANLEY sits with his back to the audience. He is talking to the father but we can't hear him. Our attention goes to EUGENE up in his room.*)

EUGENE. . . . So Stanley began his sad story. Pop never said a word. He just sat there and listened. Stanley was terrific. It was like that movie, *Abe Lincoln in Illinois.* Stanley was not only defending his principles, he was defending democracy and the United States of America. Pop must have been bleary eyed because not only did he have to deal with Stanley's principles, Nora's career, the loss of his noisemaker business, how to get Aunt Blanche married off and Laurie's fluttering heart, but at any minute there could be a knock on the door with 37 relatives from Poland showing up looking for a place to live . . . Finally, Stanley finished his story.

STAN. . . . So—either I bring in a letter of apology in the morning or I don't bother coming in . . . I know it's late. I know you're tired. But I didn't want to do anything without asking you first. (*JACK sits in silence a few moments.*)

JACK. . . . Ohh, Stanley, Stanley, Stanley!

STAN. I'm sorry, Pop.

JACK. You shouldn't have swept the dirt on his shoes.

STAN. I know.

JACK. Especially in front of other people.

STAN. I know.

JACK. He's your boss. He pays your salary. His money helps put food on our dining table.

STAN. I know, Pop.

JACK. And we don't have money to waste. Believe me when I tell you that.

STAN. I believe you, Pop.

JACK. You were sick three days last year and he only docked you a day and a half's pay, remember that?

STAN. I know. I can see what you're getting at. I'll write the letter. I'll do it tonight.

JACK. On the other hand, you did a courageous thing. You defended a fellow worker. Nobody else stood up for him, did they?

STAN. I was the only one.

JACK. That's something to be proud of. It was what you believed in. That's standing up for your principles.

STAN. That's why I didn't want to write the letter. I knew you'd understand.

JACK. The question is, can this family afford principles right now?

STAN. It would make it hard, I know.

JACK. Not just on you and me. But on your mother. On Aunt Blanche, Nora, Laurie.

STAN. Eugene.

JACK. Eugene. Eugene would have to get a part time job. Time he should be using studying books to get himself somewhere.

STAN. He wants to be a writer. He wants to go to college.

JACK. I wish I could have sent *you*. I've always been sick about that, Stanley.

STAN. I like working, Pop. I really do . . . Listen, I made up my mind. I'm going to write the letter.

JACK. I'm not saying you should.

STAN. I know. It's *my* decision. I really want to write the letter.

JACK. And how will your principles feel in the morning?

STAN. My principles feel better already. You told me you were proud of what I did. That's all I really cared about.

JACK. You know something, Stanley. I don't think there's much in college they could teach you that you don't already know.

STAN. Guess who I learned it from? . . . Thanks for talking to me, Pop. See you in the morning . . . You coming to bed?

JACK. I think I'll sit here for a while. It's the only time of day I have a few minutes to myself.

(*STANLEY nods, then bounds up the stairs to his room.
JACK sits back in his chair and closes his eyes.
STANLEY enters his room. EUGENE is writing in
his book of Memoirs.*)

EUGENE. How'd it go? Do you have to write the letter?

STAN. Yeah. (*He gets out pad and fountain pen.*)

EUGENE. I *knew* that's what he'd make you do.

STAN. He didn't *make* me do it . . . Be quiet, will ya! I
have to concentrate.

EUGENE. What are you going to say?

STAN. I don't know . . . You want to help me? You're
good at those things.

EUGENE. People used to get paid for that in the old
days. Professional letter writers.

STAN. (*indignant*) I'm not going to pay you money.

EUGENE. I don't want money.

STAN. Then what *do* you want?

EUGENE. Tell me what Nora looked like naked.

STAN. How horny can you get?

EUGENE. I don't know. What's the highest score?

STAN. . . . Alright. When we finish the letter.

EUGENE. I don't trust you. I want to get paid first.

STAN. You know, you're a real shit!

EUGENE. Don't talk like that in front of me, I'm just a
kid.

STAN. What do you want to know?

EUGENE. Everything. From the time you opened the
door.

STAN. It happened so fast.

EUGENE. That's okay. Tell it slow.

STAN. Jesus! . . . Alright . . . I heard the shower running. I waited for it to stop. I gave a few seconds for the
water to run off her body, then I knew she'd be stepping

out of the shower . . . Suddenly I just opened the door. She was standing there on the bath mat, a towel on her head and nothing else in the whole wide world.

EUGENE. Slower. Don't go so fast.

STAN. Her breasts were gorgeous. Like two peaches hanging on the vine waiting to be plucked . . . Maybe nectarines. Like two nectarines, all soft and pink and shining in the morning sun . . .

CURTAIN

ACT TWO

*Wednesday, a week later. About six thirty in the evening.
KATE comes down the stairs carrying a tray of
food. She looks a little haggard. LAURIE is lying
the sofa in the living room with a book. EUGENE
is in the back yard, sitting on the beach chair,
writing in his book of Memoirs.*

KATE. Laurie! You should see your mother. She looks
gorgeous.

LAURIE. I'm waiting for her grand entrance . . . How's
Uncle Jack?

KATE. He's resting. He ate a nice dinner. You can go
up and see him later. (*yells*) Eugene! Your father's
resting. I don't want to hear any ball playing against the
wall.

EUGENE. I'm not playing. I'm writing.

KATE. Well, do it quietly. (*She goes into the kitchen.*)

EUGENE. (*to audience*) She wants me to write quietly.
If that was the only sentence I published in my memoirs,
it would be a best seller . . . Everybody's been in a rotten
mood around here lately . . . Three days ago Pop had a
(*whispers*) heart attack. It was sort of a warning. He
passed out in the subway and a policeman had to bring
him home. He was trying to make extra money driving a
cab at nights and he just plain wore out . . . The doctor
says he has to stay home for two or three weeks but Pop
won't listen to him. Mr. Jacobson has a brother-in-law
who needs a job. He's filling in for Pop temporarily but
Pop's afraid that three weeks in bed could turn into
permanently.

65

(*STANLEY appears, coming home from work. He looks distraught. He half whispers to EUGENE.*)

STAN. I have to talk to you.

EUGENE. What's up?

STAN. Not here. In our room. Don't tell anybody.

EUGENE. What's the big secret?

STAN. Will you shut up! Wait'll I get upstairs, then follow me. (*STANLEY goes into the house.*)

EUGENE. If it's about Nora, I'm not interested. (*to audience*) I forgot to tell you, I hate my cousin Nora. She's been real snotty to everybody lately. She doesn't say hello in the morning and eats her dinner up in her room. And she's been seeing this guy Larry No Chin Clurman every night. And she's not as pretty as I thought she was . . . (*KATE comes out of the kitchen.*)

KATE. (*calls off*) Eugene! Did you bring your father his paper?

EUGENE. I'm coming. My knee hurts. I fell down the stairs at school.

KATE. Well, bring it up. Your father's waiting for it. (*goes back into kitchen*)

EUGENE. (*to audience*) If I told her I just lost both my hands in an accident she'd say "Go upstairs and wash your face with your feet" . . . I guess she's sore because she and Pop can't go to the affair at the Commodore Hotel. They had Glenn Gray and his orchestra . . . I feel sorry for her 'cause she doesn't get to go out much . . . (*He gets up, starts into house.*) And she's nervous about Frank Murphy coming over to pick up Aunt Blanche. She's angry at the whole world. (*He enters the house.*) That's why she's making lima beans for dinner.

KATE. (*crosses into living room with dish of nuts*) Would you like a cashew, Laurie?

LAURIE. Oh, thanks. (*She takes one.*) And a Brazil nut too? (*She takes one.*) And one almond? (*She takes one.*)

KATE. You must be starved. We're having dinner late tonight. We'll wait till your mother goes out. (*EUGENE limps into living room.*)

EUGENE. (*sees nuts*) Can I have some nuts, Mom?

KATE. Just one. It's for the company. (*He takes one, starts upstairs.*) We're eating in the kitchen tonight. You and Stanley help with the dishes. (*He goes upstairs.*)

KATE. (*to LAURIE*) You look all flushed. You don't have a fever, do you? (*feels LAURIE's head*) Let me see your tongue. (*LAURIE shows her her tongue.*) It's all spotted.

LAURIE. That's the cashew nut.

KATE. Don't you get sick on me too. If you're tired, I want you in bed.

LAURIE. I have a little stomach cramp. Maybe I'm getting my "ladies."

KATE. Your what?

LAURIE. My "ladies." That thing that Nora gets when she can't go in the water.

KATE. I don't think so. Not at your age. But if your stomach hurts real bad, you come and tell me. I made a nice tuna fish salad tonight. Call me when your mother comes down. (*She starts towards kitchen.*)

LAURIE. Aunt Kate! . . . Does Momma like Mr. Murphy?

KATE. I don't know, darling. I don't think she knows him very well yet.

LAURIE. Do you like him?

KATE. I never spoke to the man.

LAURIE. You called him a Cossack. Are those the kind who don't like Jewish people?

KATE. I'm sure Mr. Murphy likes your mother otherwise he wouldn't be taking her out to dinner.

LAURIE. If Mom married him, would we have to live in that dark house across the street? With that creepy woman in the window?

KATE. We're not up to that yet. Let's just get through Chardov's Restaurant first.

(She goes into the kitchen. EUGENE rushes into his room. STANLEY is lying on his bed, hands under his head, staring at the ceiling.)

EUGENE. Pop's feeling better. He threw the newspaper at me because I didn't bring him the evening edition.

STAN. *(sits up)* Lock the door.

EUGENE. *(locking door)* You look terrible. You were crying. Your eyes are all red.

STAN. I'm in trouble, Eug. I mean, real, *real* trouble. *(He takes a single cigarette out of his shirt pocket, puts it in his mouth and lights it with a match.)*

EUGENE. When did you take up smoking?

STAN. I smoke in the stock room all the time. Don't let me see you do it. It's a bad habit.

EUGENE. So how come *you* do it?

STAN. I like it.

EUGENE. What brand do you smoke?

STAN. Lucky Strikes.

EUGENE. I knew you would. That's the best brand.

STAN. Swear to God, what I tell you, you'll never tell a living soul.

EUGENE. *(raises his hand)* I take an oath on the life of the entire New York Yankees . . . What happened?

STAN. (*He paces before he can speak.*) . . . I lost my salary.

EUGENE. *What?*

STAN. The entire seventeen dollars. It's gone. I lost it.

EUGENE. Where? In the subway?

STAN. In a poker game. I lost it gambling.

EUGENE. IN A POKER GAME?

STAN. *Will you shut up??* You want to kill Pop right in his bedroom?

EUGENE. You never told me you gambled.

STAN. We would just do it at lunch hour. For pennies. I always won. A dime. A quarter. It wasn't just luck. I was really good.

EUGENE. Seventeen dollars!!

STAN. When Pop was sick, I thought I could make some extra money. To help out. So I played in this game over in the stockroom at Florsheim Shoes . . . Boy, did I learn about poker. They cleaned me out in twenty minutes . . .

EUGENE. What are you going to tell them?

STAN. I don't know. If Pop wasn't sick, I would tell him the truth. Last week he tells me how proud he is of me. He's driving a cab at nights and I'm playing poker at Florsheims. (*He puts his head down and starts to cry.*)

EUGENE. Yeah, but suppose you won? Suppose you won fifty dollars? You just had bad luck, that's all.

STAN. I had no chance against those guys. They were gamblers. They all wore black, pointy shoes with clocks on their socks . . . If Pop dies, I'll hang myself, I swear.

EUGENE. Don't talk like that. Pop isn't going to die. He ate three lamb chops tonight . . . Why don't you just say you lost the money? You had a hole in your pocket. You can tear a hole in your pocket.

STAN. I already used that one.

EUGENE. When?

STAN. In November when I lost five dollars. He said to me, "From now on, check your pockets every morning."

EUGENE. What happened to the five dollars? Did you gamble that too?

STAN. No. I gave it to a girl . . . You know. A pro.

EUGENE. A pro what? . . . A PROSTITUTE??? You went to one of those places? Holy shit!

STAN. I'm not going to warn you about that word again.

EUGENE. Is that what it costs? Five dollars?

STAN. Two fifty. I went with this guy I know. He still owes me.

EUGENE. And you never told me? What was she like? Was she pretty? How old was she?

STAN. Don't start in with me, Eugene.

EUGENE. Did she get completely naked or what?

STAN. (*furious*) Every time I get in trouble, I have to tell you what a naked girl looks like? . . . Do me a favor, Eugene. Go in the bathroom, whack off and grow up by yourself.

EUGENE. Don't get sore. If you were me, you'd ask the same questions.

STAN. Well, I never had an older brother to teach me those things. I had to do it all on my own. You don't know how lucky you are to be the younger one. You don't have the responsibilities I do. You're still in school looking up girls' dresses on the staircase.

EUGENE. I work plenty hard in school.

STAN. Yeah? Well, let me see your report card. Today's the first of the month, I know you got it. I want to see your report card.

EUGENE. I don't have to show you my report card. You're not my father.

STAN. Yes, I am. As long as Pop is sick, I am. I'm the only one in the family who's working, ain't I?

EUGENE. Really? Well, where's your salary this week, Pop?

STAN. (*grabs EUGENE in anger*) I hate you sometimes. You're nothing but a lousy shit. I help you all the time and you never help me without wanting something for it. I hate your disgusting guts.

EUGENE. (*screaming*) Not as much as I hate yours. You snore at night. You pick your toe nails. You smell up the bathroom. When I go in there I have to puke.

STAN. (*screaming back*) Give me your report card. Give it to me, God dammit, or I'll beat your face in.

EUGENE. (*starts to cry*) You want it? Here! (*He grabs it out of a book.*) Here's my lousy report card . . . you fuck!! (*He falls on the bed crying, his face to the wall. STANLEY sits on his own bed and reads the report card. There is a long silence.*)

STAN. (*softly*) . . . Four A's and a B . . . That's good. That's real good, Eugene . . . You're smart . . . I want you to go to college . . . I want you to be somebody important someday . . . Because I'm not . . . I'm no damn good. . . . I'm sorry I said those things to you.

EUGENE. (*Still faces the wall. It's too hard to look at STANLEY.*) . . . Me too . . . I'm sorry too.

(*JACK appears at the top of the stairs. He is in his pajamas, robe and slippers. He seems very shaky. He holds on to the bannister and slowly comes down the stairs. He looks around, then sees*

LAURIE and walks into the living room. His breath does not come easy.)

LAURIE. (*sees him*) Hi, Uncle Jack. Are you feeling better?

JACK. A little, darling. Your mother's not down yet?

LAURIE. No.

JACK. I wanted to see her before she goes out. (*KATE comes out of the kitchen with a bowl of fruit, sees JACK.*)

KATE. Oh, my God! Are you crazy? Are you out of your mind? You're walking down the stairs?

JACK. I'm alright. I was tired laying in that bed. I wanted to see Blanche. (*He sits down slowly.*)

KATE. How are you going to get upstairs? You think I'm going to carry you? The doctor said you're not even supposed to go to the bathroom, didn't he?

JACK. You trust doctors? My grandmother never saw one in her life, she lived to be 87.

KATE. She didn't have high blood pressure. She never fainted on the subway.

JACK. She used to faint three, four times a week. It's in our family. We're fainters. Laurie, darling. Go get your Uncle Jack a glass of ice water, please.

LAURIE. Now?

JACK. Yes. Now, sweetheart. (*LAURIE gets up and goes into kitchen.*) That child is pampered too much. You should let her do more work around the house. You don't get healthy lying on couches all day.

KATE. No. You get healthy driving cabs at night after you work nine hours cutting raincoats. You want to kill yourself, Jack? You want to leave me to take care of this family alone? Is that what you want?

JACK. You figure I'll get better faster if you make me

feel guilty? . . . I was born with enough guilt, Katey. If I need more, I'll ask you.

KATE. I'm sorry. You know me. I'm not happy unless I can worry. *My* family were worriers. Worriers generally marry fainters.

JACK. (*takes her hand, holds it*) I'm not going to leave you. I promise. If I didn't leave you for another woman, I'm certainly not going to drop dead just to leave you.

KATE. (*lets go of his hand*) What other woman? That bookkeeper, Helene?

JACK. Again with Helene? You're never going to forget that I danced with her two years in a row at the Commodore Hotel?

KATE. Don't tell me she isn't attracted to you. I noticed that right off.

JACK. What does a woman like that want with a cutter? She likes the men up front. The salesman. She's a widow. She's looking to get married.

KATE. You're an attractive man, Jack. Women like you.

JACK. Me? Attractive? You really must think I'm dying, don't you?

KATE. You don't know women like I do. Just promise me one thing. If anything ever happened with you and that Helene, let me go to my grave without hearing it.

JACK. I see. Now that you're worried about Helene, you've decided you're going to die first. (*LAURIE comes back in with glass of ice water.*)

LAURIE. I had to chop the ice. I'm all out of breath.

JACK. It's good for you, darling. It's exercise. (*He takes the ice water. NORA comes out of her room and comes bounding down the stairs.*)

NORA. (*coldly*) I'm going out. I won't be having dinner. I'll be home late. I have my key. Goodnight.

KATE. Nora! Don't you want to see how your mother looks?

NORA. I'm sure she looks beautiful. She doesn't need me to tell her.

KATE. What about Mr. Murphy? I know your mother wants him to meet you and Laurie. He'll be here any minute.

NORA. I have somebody waiting for me. I can meet Mr. Murphy some other time.

JACK. I think it would be nice if you waited, Nora. I think your mother would be very hurt if you didn't wait to say goodbye.

NORA. I'm sure that's very good advice, Uncle Jack. I know *just* how my mother feels. I'm not so sure she knows how *I* feel. (*She turns and goes out the front door. JACK and KATE look at each other.*)

KATE. Jack! What'll I do?

JACK. Leave it alone. It's between Nora and Blanche. It's something *they* have to work out.

KATE. Who is she going out with? Where does she go evey night?

LAURIE. With Larry Clurman. He borrows his father's car and takes her to the cemetery.

KATE. What cemetery?

LAURIE. Where Daddy is buried. She goes to see Daddy.

(*BLANCHE has come out of her room and appears at the head of the stairs. She is all dressed up and looks quite lovely. She comes down the stairs.*)

KATE. What'll I tell her? I don't want to spoil this evening for her. (*BLANCHE appears in the room.*)

BLANCHE. Jack? What are you doing down here?

JACK. We have company coming. Where else should I be?

BLANCHE. I looked in your room. I got scared to death.

JACK. Well, you don't look it. You look beautiful.

KATE. Ohh, Blanche. Oh, my God, Blanche, it's stunning. Like a movie star. Who's the movie star I like so much, Laurie?

LAURIE. Irene Dunne.

KATE. Like Irene Dunne.

LAURIE. I think she looks like Rosalind Russell. Maybe Carole Lombard.

JACK. I think she looks like Blanche. Blanche is prettier than all of them.

BLANCHE. I had such trouble with the makeup. I couldn't see my eyes to put on the mascara. So I had to put my glasses on. Then I couldn't get the mascara on under the glasses.

(*STANLEY gets up from his bed, goes out to the bathroom and closes door.*)

KATE. Where are your glasses? Have you got your glasses?

BLANCHE. In my purse. I thought I'd put them on in the restaurant, when I'm looking at the menu.

KATE. Make sure you do. I don't want you coming home telling me you don't know what he looks like.

BLANCHE. I'm so glad to see you up, Jack. Then you're feeling better?

JACK. It was nothing. I needed a rest, that's all. Besides, I wanted to meet this Murphy fella. A stranger comes in, he likes to meet another man. Makes him feel comfortable.

BLANCHE. Thank you, Jack. That's very thoughtful of you.

KATE. (*takes something out of her pocket*) Here. Wear this. Don't say no to me. Just put them on, Blanche. Please. (*It's a string of pearls.*)

BLANCHE. Kate! Your pearls. Your good pearls.

KATE. What are they going to do? Sit in my drawer all year? Pearls are like people. They like to go out and be seen once in a while.

BLANCHE. You were going to wear them to the affair tonight. I'm so wrapped up in myself, I forgot you're missing the affair this year.

KATE. I can afford to miss it. I don't see Jack there the whole night anyway.

JACK. Let's see how they look.

BLANCHE. I'm so nervous I'll lose them. (*She gets them on. They all look.*)

KATE. Alright. Tell me I don't have a beautiful sister.

JACK. Now I feel good. Now I feel I got my money's worth.

LAURIE. Definitely Carole Lombard.

BLANCHE. Laurie, go up and get Nora. I want to show them to Nora.

LAURIE. . . . She's not here. She left.

BLANCHE. (*looks at KATE and JACK*) What do you mean, she left? Without saying goodbye?

KATE. She had to meet somebody. She wanted to wait for you.

BLANCHE. She could have come in to my room. She knew I wanted to see her.

JACK. She'll see you when you get home. You'll look just as good at twelve o'clock.

BLANCHE. What did she say? Did she say anything?

KATE. You're going out. You're going to have a good time tonight.

BLANCHE. She's making me pay for it, isn't she? She knows she can get to me so easily . . . That's what I get for making decisions.

JACK. . . . I feel like ice cream for dessert. Laurie, you feel like ice cream for dessert?

LAURIE. Butter pecan?

JACK. Butter pecan for you, maple walnut for me. Go up and tell Eugene I want him to go to the store.

LAURIE. I'll go with him.

KATE. Don't run, darling.

JACK. Let her run. If she gets tired, she'll tell you. Let's stop worrying about each other so much. (*LAURIE knocks on EUGENE's door.*)

LAURIE. Eugene! Your father wants us to go to the store.

EUGENE. Tell him I'm sick. My stomach hurts.

LAURIE. You don't want any ice cream?

EUGENE. (*thinks*) Ice cream? Wait a minute. (*He sits up, looks out at audience.*) It's amazing how quickly you recover from misery when someone offers you ice cream.

JACK. She's only 16, Blanche. At that age they're still wrappd up in themselves.

EUGENE. How am I going to become a writer if I don't know how to suffer? Actually, I'd give up writing if I could see a naked girl while I was eating ice cream. (*He crosses out of his room and goes down the stairs with LAURIE. STANLEY comes out of the bathroom and goes back into his own room.*)

BLANCHE. What time is it?

KATE. Six thirty. He'll be here any minute. Get your

mind off Nora, Blanche. Don't wear my pearls out tonight for nothing.

JACK. Eugene! Go to Hansons. Get a half pint of butter pecan, a half pint of maple walnut, a half pint of chocolate for yourself. Kate, what do you want?

KATE. I'm in no mood for ice cream.

JACK. Get her vanilla. She'll eat it. And whatever Stanley likes.

EUGENE. I need money.

JACK. I just paid the doctor fifteen dollars. Go up to Stanley. He got paid today. Ask him for his salary.

EUGENE. (*in shock*) *What???*

KATE. Here. Here's a dollar. (*takes dollar from her pocket*) Hurry back so Laurie can meet Mr. Murphy. But don't run. (*They take the money and exit front door.*)

BLANCHE. You know what I worry about at nights? That she'll run off. That I'll wake up in the morning and she'll be gone. To Philadelphia. Or Boston. Or God knows where.

KATE. Look how the woman's going out on a date. Is that what you're going to talk about? He'll start drinking in five minutes.

BLANCHE. You think so? What'll I do if he gets drunk?

KATE. You'll come right home. Do you have money? Do you have carfare?

BLANCHE. No. I didn't take anything.

KATE. Wait here. I'll get five dollars from Stanley. Now I have something *else* to worry about. (*She starts up the stairs.*)

JACK. I could use a cup of hot tea. (*He gets up.*)

BLANCHE. Sit there. I'll make it.

JACK. We'll both make it. Keep me company. We can

hear the bell from the kitchen. (*They go off to the kitchen. KATE is at STANLEY's door. She knocks on it.*)

KATE. Stanley? Are you in there? (*She opens the door. STANLEY is lying on his bed.*) Open the window. You never get any air in this room . . . (*extends her hand*) I need five dollars for Aunt Blanche. (*He stares at the floor.*) . . . Stanley? Did you get paid today?

STAN. Yes. I got paid today.

KATE. Take out your money for the week, let me have the envelope.

STAN. (*still stares down*) I don't have it.

KATE. You don't have the envelope?

STAN. I don't have the money.

KATE. What do you mean, you don't have the money?

STAN. I mean I don't have the money. It's gone.

KATE. (*nervously, sits on the bed*) It's gone? . . . Gone where?

STAN. It's just gone. I don't have it. I can't get it back. I'm sorry. There's nothing I can do about it anymore. Just don't ask me any more questions.

KATE. What do you mean, don't ask any more questions? I want to know what happened to seventeen dollars, Stanley!

STAN. You'll tell Pop. If I tell you, you're going to tell Pop.

KATE. Why shouldn't I tell your father? Why, Stanley? I want to know what happened to that money.

STAN. I gambled it! I lost it playing poker! Alright? You happy? You satisfied now? (*He starts to weep.*)

KATE. (*Her breath goes out of her body. She sits there numb, then finally takes a breath.*) . . . I'm not going to deal with this right now. I have to get Aunt Blanche out of the house first. I have your father's health to worry about. You're going to sit in this room and you're going to think up a story. You were robbed. Somebody stole the money. I don't care who, I don't care where. That's what you're going to tell your father, because if you tell him the truth, you'll kill that man as sure as I'm sitting here . . . Tonight, after he goes to sleep, you'll meet me in the kitchen and we'll deal with this alone. (*She gets up, moves to door.*)

STAN. (*barely audible*) . . . I'm sorry.

(*She goes, closes the door. STANLEY sits there as if the life has gone out of him. KATE comes down the stairs. She crosses into the living room. She crosses to the window, looks out, and breaks into sobs. BLANCHE comes out of the kitchen. She looks around the living room.*)

BLANCHE. I left my purse in here. Without my glasses, I'm afraid to pour the tea. (*She notices KATE wiping her eyes with her handkerchief.*) Kate? . . . What is it? What's wrong?

KATE. Nothing. I'm just all nerves today.

BLANCHE. You're worried about Jack. He shouldn't have come down the stairs.

KATE. He knows he's not supposed to get out of bed. What did we need a doctor for? He doesn't listen to them.

BLANCHE. I shouldn't have asked Mr. Murphy to come over. That's the only reason he came down.

KATE. It's not just Mr. Murphy. It's Stanley, it's Eugene, it's everybody.

BLANCHE. I'm sorry about Nora. Jack told me what she said when she left.

KATE. Why don't you get your purse, Blanche. He'll be here any minute.

BLANCHE. Did Nora say anything to hurt you, Kate? I know she's been very difficult these last few days.

KATE. (*suddenly turns, angrily*) Why is it always *Nora*? Why is it only *your* problems? Do you think you're the only one in this world who has troubles? We *all* have troubles. We *all* get our equal share.

BLANCHE. (*like a slap in the face*) I'm sorry. Forgive me, Kate. I'm sorry.

KATE. Maybe you're stronger than I am, I don't know. You survived Dave's death. I don't know if I could handle it if anything happens to Jack.

BLANCHE. He'll be alright, Kate. Nothing's going to happen to him. He's still a young man. He's strong.

KATE. When Dave died, I cried for his loss. I was so angry. Angry at God for taking such a young man . . . I never realized until now what *you* must have gone through. How did you get through it, Blanche?

BLANCHE. I had you. I had Jack . . . But mostly, you live for your children. Your children keep you going.

KATE. (*almost a smile*) My Children.

BLANCHE. I wake up every morning for Nora and for Laurie.

KATE. Nora hurts you so much and you can still say that?

BLANCHE. Why? Don't you think we hurt *our* parents? You don't remember how Momma cried when Celia left home? Sure it hurts, but if you love someone, you forgive them.

KATE. Some things you forgive. Some things you never forgive. (*LAURIE comes back into the house. She has a letter in her hand.*)

LAURIE. Is the ice cream here yet?

BLANCHE. No, darling. Didn't you go with Eugene?

LAURIE. No. I was across the street in the creepy house. It's just as creepy inside.

BLANCHE. In Mr. Murphy's house? You were just in there? Why?

LAURIE. She called me from the window. The old lady. I think it's his mother. She told me she had a letter for you. I had to go inside to get it. (*She hands letter to BLANCHE.*)

KATE. What did she say to you?

LAURIE. She offered me a cookie but it was all green. I said I wasn't hungry.

(*EUGENE appears outside the house. He carries a brown paper bag with four small cartons of ice cream. BLANCHE opens the letter.*)

EUGENE. (*to audience*) "Dear Mrs. Morton, I send regrets for my son Frank. I tried to reach you earlier, then realized you had no phone. Frank will be unable to keep his dinner engagement with you this evening. Frank is in hospital as a result of an automobile accident last night and although his injuries are not serious, the consequences are. As a devoted mother I would end this letter here and forward my apologies. Despite all my son's faults, honesty and sincerity have never been his failings. He wanted me to tell you the truth. That while driving a friend's motor car, he was intoxicated and was the cause of the aforementioned accident. The truth would come out soon enough, but Frank has too much respect and fondness for you to have you hear it from some other source. I hope you will not think I am just a doting mother when I tell you my boy has a great many attributes. A great many. As soon as Frank can get out of his difficulties here we have decided to move to upstate New York where there is a clinic that can help Frank and where we have relatives with whom we can stay. Frank sends along with his regrets, his regard for a warm, intelligent, friendly and most delightful neighbor across the way . . . Yours most respectfully, Mrs. Matthew Murphy."

KATE. What is it? (*BLANCHE hands the letter to KATE.*)

BLANCHE. He's not coming. He's . . . in the hospital. (*KATE reads the letter.*)

EUGENE. (*to audience*) It was a sad letter alright, but it sure was well written. Maybe I should have been born in Ireland. (*He crosses into the house.*)

KATE. (*as she reads*) I knew it. I said it right from the begining, didn't I?

LAURIE. Why is he in the hospital?

BLANCHE. He was in a car accident . . . Oh, God. That poor woman.

LAURIE. Does that mean you're not going out to dinner?

KATE. (*nodding her head as she finishes*) It could have been you in that car with him. I warned you the first day about those people.

BLANCHE. Stop calling them "those people." They're not "those people." She's a mother, like you and me.

KATE. And what is he? Tell me what he is.

BLANCHE. He's somebody in trouble. He's somebody that needs help. For God's sakes, Kate, you don't even know the man.

KATE. I know the man. I know what they're *all* like.

BLANCHE. Who are you to talk? Are we any better? Are we something so special? We're *all* poor around here, the least we can be is charitable.

KATE. Why? What have *I* got I can afford to give

away? Am I the one who got you all dressed up for nothing? Am I the one who got your hopes up? Am I the one they're going to lock up in a jail somewhere?

LAURIE. They're going to put him in jail?

KATE. Don't talk to me about charity. Anyone else, but not me.

BLANCHE. I never said you weren't charitable.

KATE. All I did was try to help you. All I *ever* did was try to help you.

BLANCHE. I know that. Nobody cares for their family more than you do. But at least you can be sympathetic to sombody else in trouble.

KATE. Who should I care about? Who's out there watching over *me?* I did enough in my life for people. You know what I'm talking about.

BLANCHE. No, I don't. Say what's on your mind, Kate. What people?

KATE. You! Celia! Poppa, when he was sick. Everybody! . . . Don't you ask *me* what people! How many beatings from Momma did I get for things that you did? How many dresses did I go without so you could look like someone when you went out? I was the workhorse and you were the pretty one. You have no right to talk to me like that. No right.

BLANCHE. This is all about Jack, isn't it? You're blaming me for what happened.

KATE. Why do you think that man is sick today? Why did a policeman have to carry him home at two o'clock in the morning? So your Nora could have dancing lessons? So that Laurie could see a doctor every three weeks? Go on! Worry about your friend across the street, not the ones who have to be dragged home to keep a roof over your head. (*She turns away. JACK walks in from the kitchen.*)

JACK. What is this? What's going on here?

BLANCHE. (*to KATE*) Why didn't you ever tell me you felt that way?

KATE. (*turns her back to her*) I never had the time. I was too busy taking care of everyone.

JACK. What is it, Blanche? What happened? (*She hands JACK the letter. He starts to read it.*)

BLANCHE. It took all those years? It took something like that letter for you to finally get your feelings out?

KATE. I didn't need a letter . . . I just needed you to ask me. (*BLANCHE is terribly hurt and extremely vulnerable standing there.*)

BLANCHE. Laurie! Please go upstairs. This conversation isn't for you.

EUGENE. The ice cream is ready.

BLANCHE. Eugene, put the ice cream in the ice box. I have to talk to your mother. (*EUGENE goes into the kitchen.*)

JACK. (*finishes the letter*) I never spoke to the woman. They've lived in that house for three years, and I never exchanged a word with her.

KATE. (*to JACK*) What are you walking around for? If you're out of bed, at least sit in a chair.

BLANCHE. If I could take Nora and Laurie, and pack them out of this house tonight, I would do it. But I can't. I have no place to take them.

JACK. Blanche! What are you talking about? Don't say such things.

BLANCHE. (*looking straight at KATE*) If I can leave the girls with you for another few weeks, I would appreciate it. Until I can find a place of my own and then I'll send for them.

JACK. You're not sending for anybody and you're not leaving anywhere. I don't want to hear this kind of talk.

KATE. Stay out of this, Jack. Let her do what she wants.

BLANCHE. I know a woman in Manhattan Beach. I can stay with her for a few days. And then I'll find a job. I will do *anything* anybody asks me, but I will never be a burden to anyone again. (*She starts for stairs.*)

JACK. Blanche, stop this! Stop it right now. What the hell is going on here, for God's sake. Two sisters having a fight they should have had twenty-five years ago. You want to get it out, Blanche, get it out! Tell her what it's like to live in a house that isn't yours. To have to depend on somebody else to put the food on your plate every night. I know what it's like because I lived that way until I was twenty-one years old . . . Tell her, Kate, what it is to be an older sister. To suddenly be the one who has to work and shoulder all the responsibilities and not be the one who gets the affection and the hugs when you were the only one there. You think I don't see it with Stanley and Eugene! With Nora and Laurie? You think I don't hear the fights that go on up in those rooms night after night. Go on, Kate! Scream at her! Yell at her. Call her names, Blanche. Tell her to go to hell for the first time in your life . . . And when you both got it out of your systems, give each other a hug and go have dinner. My lousy ice cream is melting, for God's sake. (*There is a long silence.*)

BLANCHE. I love you both very much. No matter what Kate says to me, I will never stop loving her . . . But I have to get out. If I don't do it now, I will lose whatever self-respect I have left. For people like us sometimes the only thing we really own is our dignity . . . and when I grow old, I would like to have as much as Mrs. Matthew Murphy across the street. (*She turns and goes up the stairs, disappearing into her room.*)

JACK. . . . What did it, Kate? Something terrible must have happened to you tonight for you to behave like this. It wasn't Blanche. It was something else. What was it, Kate?

KATE. (*stares out the window*) Tell the kids to come down in five minutes. We're eating in the kitchen, tonight. (*She walks into the kitchen. JACK stands there, staring after her. EUGENE comes out of the kitchen. The father passes him.*)

JACK. Get Stanley and Laurie. Dinner is in five minutes. (*JACK goes into the kitchen. EUGENE crosses the room to the stairs and up towards his bedroom.*)

EUGENE. (*to audience*) It was the first day in my life I didn't get blamed for what just happened. I felt real sorry for everybody, but as long as I wasn't to blame, I didn't feel all *that* bad about things. That's when I realized I had a selfish streak in me. I sure hope I grow out of it. (*He enters his bedroom. To STANLEY:*) Aunt Blanche is leaving.

STAN. (*sits up*) For where?

EUGENE. (*sits on his own bed*) To stay with some woman in Manhattan Beach. She and Mom just had a big fight. She's going to send for Laurie and Nora when she gets a job.

STAN. What did they fight about?

EUGENE. I couldn't hear it all. I think Mom sorta blames Aunt Blanche for Pop having to work so hard.

STAN. (*hits pillow with his fist*) Oh, God! . . . Did Mom say anything about me? About how I lost my salary?

EUGENE. You told her? Why did you tell her? I came up with twelve terrific lies for you. (*STANLEY opens his drawer, puts on a sweater.*)

STAN. How much money do you have?

EUGENE. Me? I don't have any money.

STAN. (*puts another sweater over the first one*) The hell you don't. You've got money in your cigar box. How much do you have?

EUGENE. I got a dollar twelve. It's my life's savings.

STAN. Let me have it. I'll pay it back, don't worry. (*He puts a jacket over sweaters, then gets a fedora from closet and puts it on. EUGENE takes cigar box from under his bed, opens it.*)

EUGENE. What are you putting on all those things for?

STAN. In case I have to sleep out tonight. I'm leaving, Gene. I don't know where I'm going yet, but I'll write to you when I get there.

EUGENE. You're leaving home?

STAN. When I'm gone, you tell Aunt Blanche what happened to my salary. Then she'll know why Mom was so angry. Tell her please not to leave because it was all my fault, not Mom's. Will you do that? (*He takes coins out of cigar box.*)

EUGENE. I have eight cents worth of stamps, if you want that too.

STAN. Thanks. (*picks up a small medal*) What's this?

EUGENE. The medal you won for the hundred yard dash two years ago.

STAN. From the Police Athletic League. I didn't know you still had this.

EUGENE. You gave it to me. You can have it back if you want it.

STAN. It's not worth anything.

EUGENE. It is to me.

STAN. Sure. You can keep it.

EUGENE. Thanks . . . Where will you go?

STAN. I don't know. I've been thinking about joining the army. Pop says we'll be at war in a couple of years anyway. I could be a sergeant or something by the time it starts.

EUGENE. If it lasts long enough, I could join too. Maybe we can get in the same outfit.

STAN. You don't go in the army unless they come and get you. You go to college. You hear me? Promise me you'll go to college.

EUGENE. I'll probably have to stay home and work, if you leave. We'll need the money.

STAN. I'll send home my paycheck every month. A sergeant in the army makes real good dough . . . Well, I better get going.

EUGENE. (*on the verge of tears*) What do you have to leave for?

STAN. Don't start crying. They'll hear you.

EUGENE. They'll get over it. They won't stay mad at you forever. I was mad at you and *I* got over it.

STAN. Because of me, the whole family is breaking up. Do you want Nora to end up like one of those cheap boardwalk girls?

EUGENE. I don't care. I'm not in love with Nora anymore.

STAN. Well, you *should* care. She's your cousin. Don't turn out to be like me.

EUGENE. I don't see what's so bad about you.

STAN. (*looks at him*) . . . Take care of yourself, Eug. (*They embrace. He opens the door, looks around, then back to EUGENE.*) If you ever write a story about me, call me Hank. I always liked the name Hank. (*He goes, closing the door behind him. EUGENE sits there in silence for a while, then turns to the audience.*)

EUGENE. (*to audience*) I guess there comes a time in

everybody's life when you say, "this very moment is the end of my childhood." When Stanley closed the door, I knew that moment had come to me . . . I was scared. I was lonely. And I hated my mother and father for making him so unhappy. Even if they were right, I still hated them . . . I even hated Stanley a little because he left me there to grow up all by myself. (*KATE yells up.*)

KATE. Eugene! Laurie! It's dinner. I'm not waiting all night.

EUGENE. (*to audience*) And I hated her for leaving Stanley's name out when she called us for dinner. I don't think parents really know how cruel they can be sometimes . . . (*a beat*) At dinner I tried to tell them about Stanley but I just couldn't get the words out . . . I left the table without even having my ice cream . . . If it was suffering I was after, I was beginning to learn about it. (*KATE and JACK come out of the kitchen, heading upstairs.*)

JACK. It's ten o'clock, where is Stanley so late?

KATE. Never mind Stanley. You should have been in bed an hour ago.

JACK. Why won't you tell me what happened between you and that boy?

KATE. I'm tired, Jack. I've had enough to deal with for one day.

JACK. I want him to go to temple with me on Saturday. They stop going for three or four weeks, they forget their religion altogether. (*They go into bedroom.*)

EUGENE. The house became quieter than I ever heard it before. Aunt Blanche was in her room packing, Pop and Mom were in their bedroom and I had to talk to somebody or else I'd go crazy. I didn't have much choice. (*He crosses over to her room and knocks on the door.*) Laurie? It's Eugene. Can I come in?

LAURIE. What do you want? I'm reading.

EUGENE. (*He opens the door.*) I just want to talk to you.

LAURIE. I didn't say yes, did I?

EUGENE. Well, I'm already in so it's too late . . . What are you reading?

LAURIE. *The Citadel* by A.J. Cronin.

EUGENE. I read it. It's terrific . . . I hear your mother's leaving in the morning.

LAURIE. We're going too as soon as she finds a job.

EUGENE. I can't believe it. I'm going to be the only one left here.

LAURIE. You mean you and Stanley.

EUGENE. Stanley's gone. He's not coming back. I think he's going to join the army.

LAURIE. You mean he ran away?

EUGENE. No. Only kids run away. When you're Stanley's age, you just leave.

LAURIE. He didn't say goodbye?

EUGENE. My parents don't even know about it. I'm going to tell them now.

LAURIE. I wonder if I'll have to go to a different school.

EUGENE. You'll have to make all new friends.

LAURIE. I don't care. I don't have any friends here anyway.

EUGENE. Because you're always in the house. You never go out.

LAURIE. I can't because of my condition.

EUGENE. You don't look sick to me. Do you *feel* sick?

LAURIE. No. But my mother tells me I am.

EUGENE. I don't trust parents anymore.

LAURIE. Why would she lie to me?

EUGENE. To keep you around. Once they find out Stanley's gone, they're going to handcuff me to my bed.

LAURIE. I wouldn't leave my mother anyway. Even when I'm older. Even if I get married. I'll never leave my mother.

EUGENE. Yeah? Mr. Murphy across the street never left his mother. And he ended up going to jail.

LAURIE. None of this would have happened if my father was alive.

EUGENE. How did you feel when he died?

LAURIE. I don't remember. I cried a lot because I saw my mother crying.

EUGENE. I would hate it if my father died. Especially with Stanley gone. We'd probably have to move out of this house.

LAURIE. Well . . . then you and your mother could come and live with us.

EUGENE. So if we all end up living together, what's the point in breaking up now?

LAURIE. I don't know. I have to finish reading. (*She goes back to her book. EUGENE gets up and looks at the audience.*)

EUGENE. You don't get too far talking to Laurie. Sometimes I think the flutter in her heart is really in her brain. (*He crosses out of room, closes door and heads down the stairs. To audience.*) . . . I went into their bedroom and broke the news about Stanley. The monumental news that their eldest son had run off, probably to get killed in France fighting for his country. My mother said, "Go to bed. He'll be home when it gets cold out" . . . I couldn't believe it. Their own son. It was then that I suspected that Stanley and I were adopted . . . They finally went to bed and I waited out on the front steps until it got cold . . . but Stanley never showed up.

(*He goes out the front door. It is later that night, after*

*midnight. We see NORA enter the front yard.
BLANCHE comes down the stairs in a nightgown
and a robe. She waits at the foot of the stairs as
NORA comes into the house and sees her.*)

BLANCHE. I wanted to talk to you.
NORA. Now? It's late.
BLANCHE. I know it's late. We could have talked
earlier if you didn't come home at twelve o'clock at
night. (*BLANCHE crosses into the living room. NORA
follows her in and stands in the doorway.*)
NORA. How was your dinner?
BLANCHE. I didn't go. Mr. Murphy was in an acci-
dent.
NORA. I'm sorry. Is he alright?
BLANCHE. He's got his problems, like the rest of us . . .
I was very hurt that you left tonight without saying
goodbye.
NORA. I was late. Someone was waiting for me.
BLANCHE. So was I. You knew it was important to
me.
NORA. I'm not feeling very well.
BLANCHE. You purposely left without seeing me.
You've never done that before.
NORA. Can we talk about this in the morning?
BLANCHE. I won't be here in the morning.
NORA. Then tomorrow night.
BLANCHE. I'm leaving, Nora. I'm moving out in the
morning.
NORA. What are you talking about?
BLANCHE. Aunt Kate and I had a fight tonight. We
said some terrible things to each other. Things that have
been bottled up since we were children. I'm going to stay

with my friend Louise, in Manhattan Beach until I can find a job. Then I'll send for you and Laurie.

NORA. I can't believe it. You mean it's alright for you to leave *us* but it wasn't alright for me to leave *you?*

BLANCHE. I was never concerned about your leaving *me.* It was your future I was worrying about.

NORA. It was *my* future. Why couldn't *I* have something to say about it?

BLANCHE. Maybe I was wrong, I don't know. I never made the decisions for the family. Your father did. Everyone always took care of me. My mother, my sisters, your father, even you and Laurie. I've been a very dependent person all my life.

NORA. Maybe that's all I'm asking for. To be *in*dependent.

BLANCHE. (*sternly*) You *earn* your independence. You don't take it at the expense of others. Would that job even be offered to you if somebody in this family hadn't paid for those dancing lessons and kept a roof over your head and clothes on your back? If anyone's going to pay back Uncle Jack it'll be me—doing God knows what, I don't know—but one thing I'm sure of. I'll *steal* before I let my daughter show that man one ounce of ingratitude or disrespect.

NORA. So I have to give up the one chance I may never get again, is that it? I'm the one who has to pay for what you couldn't do with your own life.

BLANCHE. (*angrily*) What right do you have to judge me like that?

NORA. *Judge* you? I can't even talk to you. I don't exist to you. I have tried so hard to get close to you but there was never any room. Whatever you had to give went to Daddy, and when he died, whatever was left you gave to—(*She turns away.*)

BLANCHE. What? Finish what you were going to say.

NORA. . . . I have been jealous my whole life of Laurie because she was lucky enough to be born sick. I could never turn a light on in my room at night or read in bed because Laurie always needed her precious sleep. I could never have a friend over on the weekends because Laurie was always resting. I used to pray I'd get some terrible disease or get hit by a car so I'd have a leg all twisted or crippled and then once, maybe just once, *I'd* get to crawl into bed next to you on a cold rainy night and talk to you and hold you until I fell asleep in your arms . . . just once . . . (*She is in tears.*)

BLANCHE. My God, Nora . . . is that what you think of me?

NORA. Is it any worse than what you think of me?

BLANCHE. (*hesitates, trying to recover*) . . . I'm not going to let you hurt me, Nora. I'm not going to let you tell me that I don't love you or that I haven't tried to give you as much as I gave Laurie . . . God knows I'm not perfect because enough angry people in this house told me so tonight . . . But I am *not* going to be a doormat for all the frustrations and unhappiness that you or Aunt Kate or anyone else wants to lay at my feet . . . I did *not* create this Universe. I do *not* decide who lives and dies, or who's rich or poor or who feels loved and who feels deprived. If you feel cheated that Laurie gets more than you, than I feel cheated that I had a husband who died at thirty-six. And if you keep on feeling that way, you'll end up like me . . . with something much worse than loneliness or helplessness and that's self-pity. Believe me, there is no leg that's twisted or bent that is more crippling than a human being who thrives on his own misfortunes . . . I am sorry, Nora, that you feel unloved and I will do everything I can to change it except apologize for it. I am tired of apologizing. After a while it becomes your life's work and it doesn't bring any money into the house . . . If it's taken your pain and Aunt Kate's anger to get me to start living again, then God will give me the strength to make it up to you, but I will *not* go back to being that frightened, helpless woman that *I* created! . . . I've already buried someone I love. Now it's time to bury someone I hate.

NORA. . . . I didn't ask you to hate yourself. I just asked you to love me.

BLANCHE. I do, Nora. Oh, God, why can't I make that clear to you?

NORA. I feel so terrible.

BLANCHE. Why?

NORA. Because I think I hurt you and I still want that job with Mr. Beckman.

BLANCHE. I know you do.

NORA. But I can't have it, can I?

BLANCHE. How can I answer that without you thinking I'm still depriving you?

NORA. I don't know . . . Maybe you just did.

BLANCHE. I hope so, Nora. I pray to God it's so. (*KATE appears coming down the stairs.*)

KATE. I heard voices downstairs. I didn't know who it was.

BLANCHE. I'm sorry if we woke you . . . Go on up to bed, Nora. We'll talk again in the morning.

NORA. Alright . . . Goodnight, Aunt Kate. (*NORA goes upstairs.*)

KATE. Is she alright?

BLANCHE. Yes.

KATE. She's not angry anymore?

BLANCHE. No, Kate. No one's angry anymore. (*NORA goes into bedroom.*) I just explained everything to Nora. The girls will help you with all the housework while I'm gone. Laurie's strong enough to do her share. I've kept her being a baby long enough.

KATE. They've never been any trouble to me, those girls. Never.

BLANCHE. I'll try to take them on the weekends if I can . . . It's late. We could both use a good night's sleep. (*She starts out of the room.*)

KATE. Blanche! . . . Don't go! (*BLANCHE stops.*) I feel badly enough for what I said. Don't make me feel any worse.

BLANCHE. Everything you said to me tonight was true, Kate. I wish to God you said it years ago.

KATE. What would I do without you? Who else do I have to talk to all day? What friends do I have in this neighborhood? Even the Murphys across the street are leaving.

BLANCHE. You and I never had any troubles before tonight, Kate. . . . It's the girls I'm thinking of now. We have to be together. The three of us. It's what they want as much as I do.

KATE. Alright. I'm not saying you shouldn't have it. But you're not going to find a job overnight. Apartments are expensive. While you're looking, why do you have to live with strangers in Manhatten Beach?

BLANCHE. Louise isn't a stranger. She's a good friend.

KATE. To me good friends are strangers. But sisters are sisters.

BLANCHE. I'm afraid of becoming comfortable here. I I don't get out now, when will I ever do it?

KATE. The door is open. Go whenever you want. When you got the job, when you find the apartment, I'll help you move. I can look with you. I know how to bargain with these landlords.

BLANCHE. (*smiles*) You wouldn't mind doing that?

KATE. They see a woman all alone, they take advantage of you . . . I'll find out what they're asking for the Murphy place. It couldn't be expensive, she never cleaned it.

BLANCHE. How independent can I become if I live right across the street forom you?

KATE. Far enough away for you to close your own door, and close enough for me not to feel so lonely. (*BLANCHE looks at her with great warmth, crosses to KATE and embraces her. They hold on dearly.*)

BLANCHE. If I lived on the moon, you would still be close to me, Kate.

KATE. I'll tell Jack. He wouldn't go to sleep until I promised to come up with some good news.

BLANCHE. I suddenly feel so hungry.

KATE. Of course. You haven't had dinner. Come on. I'll fix you some scrambled eggs. (*heading towards kitchen*)

BLANCHE. I'll make them. I'm an independent woman now.

KATE. With your eyes, you'll never get the eggs in the pan.

(*They exit into kitchen. EUGENE appears in the front yard. He is carrying two bags of groceries. It is late afternoon. He stops to talk to audience.*)

EUGENE. (*to audience*) . . . So Aunt Blanche decided to stay while she was looking for a job, Nora went back to school the next morning, gave me a big smile and her legs looked as creamy white as ever. Laurie was asked to take out the garbage but she quickly got a 'flutter' in her heart, so I had to do it. Life was back to normal. (*He goes into the house. KATE comes out of the kitchen.*)

KATE. Eugene! Go back to Greenblatts. I need flour.

EUGENE. How much? A teaspoonful? (*She glares at him, takes the bags and goes back into the kitchen. He turns to audience.*) . . . Stanley didn't come home that night and even though Mom didn't say anything, I knew she was plenty worried . . . She told Pop how Stanley lost the money playing poker and from the sounds coming out of their room, I figured Stanley should forget about the army and try for the Foreign Legion. (*STANLEY appears down the street.*) And then all of a sudden, the next night about dinner time, he came back. I was never so happy to see anyone in my whole life.

STAN. Hi! (*looks around*) Where's Mom and Pop?

EUGENE. Mom's in the kitchen cooking. Pop's upstairs with his prayer book. They figured if God didn't bring you home, maybe her potato pancakes would . . . What happened? Did you join up?

STAN. I came pretty close. I passed the physical one two three.

EUGENE. I knew you would.

STAN. They were giving me cigarettes, doughnuts, the whole sales pitch. I mean they really wanted me.

EUGENE. I'll bet.

STAN. But then, just as I was about to sign my name, I stopped cold. I put down the pen and said, "I'm sorry. Maybe some other time" . . . and walked out.

EUGENE. How come?

STAN. I couldn't do it to Pop. Right now he needs me more than the army does . . . I knew Mom didn't really mean it when she said she'd never forgive me for losing the money, but if I walked out on the family now, maybe she never would.

EUGENE. Gee, I thought you'd be halfway to training camp by now . . . but I'm real glad you're home, Stan. (*They stand there looking at each other for a moment . . . KATE crosses out of the kitchen to the yard.*)

KATE. Eugene. I need a pint of sweet cream. And some more sugar.

EUGENE. Stanley's home.

STAN. Hello, Mom.

KATE. (*looks at him, then to EUGENE*) Get a two pound bag. I want to bake a chocolate cake.

EUGENE. A two pound bag from Greenblatt's? I'll need identification. (*He looks at STANLEY, then goes.*)

KATE. (*to STANLEY*) Are you staying for dinner?

STAN. I'm staying as long as you'll let me stay.

KATE. Why wouldn't I let you stay?? This is your home. (*KATE crosses into the house, STANLEY follows. JACK comes down the stairs and crosses to his favorite chair. He opens up his paper.*) . . . Your father's been very worried. I think you owe him some sort of explanation.

STAN. I was just about to do that. (*KATE looks at him, wants to reach out to touch him, but can't seem to do it. She goes back into the kitchen as STANLEY crosses into the living room.*) Hi, Pop. How you feeling? (*JACK doesn't turn. He keeps reading his newspaper.*) . . . I'm sorry about not coming home last night . . . I know it was wrong. I just didn't know how to tell you about the money . . . I know it doesn't help to say I'll never do it again, because I won't. I swear. Never . . . (*He takes money out of his pocket.*) I've got three dollars. Last night I went over to Dominick's Bowling Alley and I set pins till midnight and I could make another six on the weekend, so that makes nine. I'll get the seventeen dollars back, Pop, I promise . . . I'm not afraid of hard work. That's the one thing you taught me. Hard work and principles. That's the code I'm going to live by for the rest of my life . . . So—if you have anything you want to say to me, I'd be very glad to listen. (*He stands there and waits.*)

JACK. (*still looking at paper*) Did you read the paper tonight, Stanley?

STAN. No, Pop.

JACK. There's going to be a war. A terrible war, Stanley.

STAN. I know, Pop. (*He moves into the room, faces his father.*)

JACK. The biggest war the world has ever seen. And it frightens me. We're still not over the last one yet, and already they're starting another one.

STAN. We don't talk about it much in the store because of Mr. Stroheim being German and all.

JACK. My brother, Michael, was killed in the last War. I've told you that.

STAN. You showed me his picture in uniform.

JACK. He was nineteen years old. The day he left, he didn't look any older than Eugene . . . He was killed the second week he was overseas . . .

STAN. I know.

JACK. They didn't take me because I was 16 years old, both parents were dead, and I lived with my Aunt Rose and Uncle Maury. They had two sons in the navy, both of them wounded, both of them decorated.

STAN. Uncle Leon and Uncle Paul, right?

JACK. (*nods*) My brother would have been 45 years

old this month. He was a handsome boy. Good athlete, good dancer, good everything. I idolized him. Like Eugene idolizes you.

STAN. No, he doesn't.

JACK. He does, believe me. I hear him outside, talking to his friends. "My brother this, my bother that" . . . Brothers can talk to each other the way fathers and sons never do . . . I never knew a thing about girls until my brother taught me. Isn't it like that with you and Eugene?

STAN. Yeah, I tell him a few things.

JACK. That's good. I'm glad you're so close . . . I missed all that when Michael went away . . . That's why I'm glad you didn't do anything foolish last night. I was afraid maybe you'd run away. I hear you talking with Eugene sometimes about the army. That day will come soon enough, I'm afraid.

STAN. I did think about it. It was on my mind.

JACK. Don't you know, Stanley, there's nothing you could ever do that was so terrible, I couldn't forgive you. I know why you gambled. I know how terrible you feel. It was foolish, you know that already. I've lost money gambling in my time, I know what it's like.

STAN. You did?

JACK. You're so surprised? You think your father's a perfect human being? Some day I'll tell you some other things I did that wasn't so perfect. Not even your mother knows. If you grow up thinking I was perfect, you'll hate yourself for every mistake you ever make. Don't be so hard on yourself. That's what you've got a mother and father to do.

STAN. You're not hard on me. You're always fair.

JACK. I try to be. You're a good son, Stanley. You

don't even realize that. We have men in our cutting room who haven't spoken to their sons in five, six years. Boys who have no respect for anyone, including themselves; who haven't worked a day in their lives, or who've brought their parents a single day's pleasure. Thank God, I could never say that about you, Stanley.

STAN. I gambled away seventeen dollars and you're telling me how terrific I am.

JACK. Hey, wait a minute. Don't get the wrong idea. If you were home last night when your mother told me, I would have thrown you and your clothes out the window. Today I'm calmer. Today I read the newspaper. Today I'm afraid for all of us.

STAN. I understand.

JACK. After dinner tonight, you apologize to your mother and give her the three dollars.

STAN. I will.

JACK. And apologize to your Aunt Blanche because she was worried about you too.

STAN. I will.

JACK. And you can thank your brother as well. He came into my bedroom this afternoon and told me how badly you felt. He was almost in tears himself. The way he pleaded your case, I thought I had Clarence Darrow in the room.

STAN. Eugene's a terrific kid.

JACK. Alright. Go wash up and get ready for dinner. And tonight, you and I are going to go out in the back yard and I'm going to teach you how to play poker.

STAN. (*smiles*) Terrific! (*He turns to go when KATE comes out of the kitchen.*)

KATE. Is Eugene back yet?

STAN. No, Mom.

KATE. You look tired. Did you get any sleep?

STAN. I got enough. I slept at a friend's house. Can I talk to you after dinner, Mom?

KATE. Where am I going? To a night club?

STAN. I'll wash up and be right down. (*He turns and starts up the stairs.*)

KATE. Stanley! . . . You didn't join anything did you?

STAN. No, Mom.

KATE. You've got time yet. The family's growing up fast enough.

STAN. Yes, Mom. (*He turns and rushes up the stairs. KATE turns and looks at JACK.*)

JACK. It's alright. Everything is alright.

KATE. Who said it wasn't? Didn't I say he'd be home? (*calls up*) Laurie! Call your sister. Time to set the table. (*EUGENE comes running into the house with a small bag and some letters.*)

EUGENE. (*out of breath*) I just broke the world's record to Greenblatt's. Next year I'm entering the Grocery Store Olympics. Here's some mail for you, Pop.

KATE. Is that my sweet cream?

EUGENE. Never spilled a drop. The perfect run. (*She takes the bag and goes into the kitchen.*) Where's Stanley?

JACK. (*takes mail*) He's cleaning up. (*looks at mail*) Oh my God, I've got jury duty next week. (*He sits and opens up a letter. EUGENE rushes up the stairs and runs into his room. STANLEY is taking off his two sweaters.*)

EUGENE. (*closing the door*) Are you back in the family?

STAN. Yeah. Everything's great.

EUGENE. Terrific . . . You want to take a walk on the

boardwalk tonight? See what's doing?

STAN. I can't tonight. I'm busy.

EUGENE. Doing what?

STAN. I'm playing poker.

EUGENE. Poker? Are you serious?

STAN. Yeah. Right after dinner.

EUGENE. I don't believe you.

STAN. I swear to God! I got a poker game tonight.

EUGENE. You're crazy! You're genuinely crazy, Stanley . . . If you lose, I'm not sticking up for you this time.

STAN. If you don't tell anybody, I'll give you a present.

EUGENE. What kind of present?

STAN. Are you going to tell?

EUGENE. No. What's my present? (*STANLEY takes something wrapped in a piece of paper out of his jacket and hands it to EUGENE.*)

STAN. Here. It's for you. Don't leave it lying around the room. (*EUGENE starts to open it. It's post card size.*)

EUGENE. What is it?

STAN. Open it slowly. (*EUGENE does.*) Slower than that . . . Close your eyes. (*EUGENE does. It is unwrapped.*) Now look! (*EUGENE looks. His eyes almost pop open.*)

EUGENE. OH, MY GOD!! . . . SHE'S NAKED! YOU CAN SEE *EVERYTHING!!*

STAN. Lower your voice. You want to get caught with a thing like that?

EUGENE. Where did you get it? Who is she?

STAN. She's French. That's how *all* the women are in Paris.

EUGENE. I can't believe I'm looking at this? You mean

some girl actually *posed* for this? She just laid there and let some guy take a picture? (*BLANCHE comes out of kitchen.*)

BLANCHE. Laurie! Nora! Time for dinner. (*NORA and LAURIE come out of their room.*)

STAN. It belongs to the guy who owes me two and a half bucks. I can keep it until he pays me back.

EUGENE. Don't take the money. Let him keep it for a while. (*He lays back on the bed, staring at the picture. NORA and LAURIE go down the stairs as KATE comes out of the kitchen with plates and starts to set up the table.*)

STAN. That's my appreciation for being a good buddy.

EUGENE. Anytime you need a favor, just let me know.

STAN. Put it in a safe spot. Come on. It's dinner.

EUGENE. In a minute. I'll be down in a minute.

(*He lays there, eyes transfixed. STANLEY starts down the stairs. NORA and LAURIE set out napkins and utensils. BLANCHE starts to arrange the chairs. JACK, with letter in his hand, gets up, looking excited, starts into dining room.*)

JACK. Kate? Where's Kate?

KATE. Don't run. You're always running.

JACK. (*holds up letter*) It's a letter from London. My cousin Sholem got out. They got out of Poland. They're free, Kate.

BLANCHE. Thank God!

JACK. His wife, his mother, all four children. They're sailing for New York tomorrow. They'll be here in a week.

KATE. In a week?

LAURIE. Do they speak English?

JACK. I don't think so. A few words, maybe. (*to KATE*) They had to sell everything. They took only what they could carry.

STAN. Where will they stay?

JACK. Well, I'll have to discuss it with the family. Some with Uncle Leon, Uncle Paul—

KATE. With us. We can put some beds in the dining room. It's easier to eat in the kitchen anyway.

BLANCHE. The little ones can stay with Laurie. Nora can sleep with me, can't you, dear?

NORA. (*pleased*) Of course, Momma.

STAN. Don't worry about money, Pa. I'm going to hit Mr. Stroheim for that raise.

JACK. They got out. That's all that's important. They got out. (*JACK sits down at table to reread the letter. NORA, STANLEY and LAURIE look over his shoulder. BLANCHE and KATE set the table.*)

KATE. (*yells up*) Eugene! We're all waiting for you!

EUGENE. (*calls down*) Be right there! I just have to write down something. (*He looks at photo again, then picks up fountain pen and his Memoir book and begins to write.*) ... "October the second, six twenty five P.M. ... A momentous moment in the life of I, Eugene Morris Jerome ... I have seen the Golden Palace of the Himalayas ... Puberty is over. Onwards and upwards ... !"

CURTAIN

FURNITURE & PROPS

Beach chair
Sofa w/3 pillows
Arm chair
Radiator with cover on top
Dining table
7 dining chairs plus extra—total of 8
Breakfront
Radio table
Alcove table
Magazine rack
Kitchen table
2 kitchen chairs
Stove
Sink
Ice box
Master bedroom
  Bed
  Side table
Boy's room
  2 beds
  Chest
Girl's room
  2 beds
  2 chests
  1 vanity table
  1 vanity bench
Blanche's room
  Bed
  Side table
Floor lamp—living room
Floor lamp—master bedroom
Table lamp—boy's room

Table lamp — girl's room
Small table lamp
   Vanity table
   Blanche room
   Alcove table
Glasses for Blanche and Laurie
Edibles
   Applesauce
   String beans (canned cut green beans)
   Lettuce
   Raisins
   Instant coffee
   Tea
   Assorted nuts (Planters deluxe mixed nuts)
   Oatmeal cookies
   Lemons
   Light & dark pumpernickel bread
   Dill pickle chips
   Mustard
   Ketchup
   Sugar cubes
   Cigarettes (whatever Stanley smokes)
Dressing for boy's room
   Alarm clock
   Small globe
Girl's room
   Books
   Book end
   Vanity things
   Stuffed animal
Dressing for breakfront
   Glasses
   Silver
   Etc.

Medicine bottle
Towel
Cigar box
Assorted coins
Stamps
Medal
Pencils (at least 4)
Note pads
Penknife
Report cards
French postcards
Cigarettes
Box matches
2 large grocery bags w/handles — full
2 lb bag sugar ⎫
2 bags w/ice cream ⎬ All brown
1 bag w/butter ⎭
Pint bottle cream
Rye bread (not eaten)
Mrs. Murphy letter
1 large box ⎫
1 medium box ⎬ For Jack Act 1
Assorted seashells
Small glass bowl (goes on top of radiator)
Wooden hangers for closet
2 coats (never worn) ⎫
2 empty shoe boxes ⎬ Dressing
Scrapbook w/photos
Assorted letters plus
    1 — Rosalyn Weiner
    2 — Jury duty
    3 — Cousin Sholem
2 bread platters

1 — w/sliced bread } Not eaten
1 — w/unsliced bread
14 dinner plates plus extras
14 water glasses plus extras
7 drinking glasses (smaller) plus extras
14 knives, forks, spoons plus extras
6 cups & saucers plus extras
7 dessert bowls plus extras
Sugar bowl plus extras
Butter dish plus extras
4 large serving bowls plus extras
3 condiment dishes plus extras
4 tablespoons plus extras
1 set serving fork and spoon
1 large serving platter plus extras
Cookie jar or tin
Roller skate
Porcelain sink and bucket or crash box
5 pitchers
    1 — water I
    1 — water I
    1 — lemonade I
    1 — water II
    1 — water II
Nut dish
Laundry basket
Bundle of clothes
    Apron
    4 T-shirts
    1 pair shorts
    3 pair socks
Pot w/potatoes (cotton)
Potatoe masher

Coffee pot
Small tea pot
2 trays
   1 – small
   1 – large
Sock
Baseball glove
Composition book
3 white baseballs
4 taped baseballs
Sewing machine
Material to sew
Sewing basket
Fruit bowl w/plastic fruit
2 wine glasses
4 shot glasses
1 whiskey glass
Pewter cream and sugar bowl
14 napkins
2 sets of pearls
   1 – for Kate
   1 – extra
5 dollar bills
   3 – Stanley
   1 – Kate
   1 – extra
Lace table cloth
Act 1 table cloth
Act 2 table cloth
2 candlesticks
2 candles
Act 1 newspaper
Act 2 newspaper
Assorted magazines

Assorted books
5 framed photographs
   3—alcove table
   2—on chests in girl's room
Assorted dressing for bookshelves and kitchen

COSTUME PLOT

EUGENE

ACT I
  brown corduroy knickers with brown belt
  blue print cotton shirt
  brown stripe sweater vest
  maroon tie
  black high top sneakers
  brown argyle knee socks
  navy baseball cap

ACT II
  dark brown wool knickers with brown belt
  brown on white windowpane check shirt
  olive green sweater vest
  maroon tie from Act I
  green argyle knee socks
  black sneakers from Act I
  brown knickers from Act I
  blue cotton knit pullover shirt
  green argyle socks from II-1
  multicolored striped pullover sweater
  navy baseball cap from Act I

JACK

ACT I
  "A" shirt and brown socks
  off white dress shirt
  brown suit
  maroon tie

gray fedora
tan handkerchief
black shoes
wedding band

ACT II
brown striped flannel pajamas
brown leather slippers
gray and tan houndstooth check robe
blue print pajamas
brown slippers and gray robe from II-1

STANLEY

ACT I
gray trousers with brown belt and striped suspenders
brown on white check shirt
tan print necktie with gold tie bar
tan tweed cap
maroon and cream wool baseball jacket
black shoes
wristwatch
T-shirt and brown socks

ACT II
trousers, jacket, shoes, cap, watch from Act I
off white dress shirt
maroon tie with gold tie bar
During Act II he will add brown and white sweater vest
and gray pullover sweater and tan fedora.

KATE

ACT I
rust flowered dress
yellow and beige short apron with yellow handker-
    chief in pocket
brown shoes
flesh lisle stockings and garters
white slip
gold watch and wedding band

ACT II
rust linen dress
yellow bib apron with handkerchief in pocket
purple bathrobe
purple slippers
rust dress from II-1
brown shoes
tan cardigan sweater vest

BLANCHE

ACT I
white slip, flesh lisle stockings, garter belt, flesh
    pantihose
navy blue skirt
green sweater
gray print smock with handkerchief in pocket and
    tape measure around neck
navy blue shoes

ACT II
aqua dress with white collar
white shoes

white straw hat
white gloves
white purse with green handkerchief inside
pearls
print flannel nightgown
purple chenille robe
blue and pink crocheted slippers
blue skirt from Act I
peach blouse
blue shoes from Act I

NORA

ACT I
bra, camisole, tap pants, white ankle socks
peach short sleeve pullover sweater
beige checked skirt
rust cardigan sweater
black and white saddle shoes
gold locket, green beads
pink flowered print bathrobe

ACT II
pink flowered print dress
white beaded purse
tan shoes
locket from Act I
skirt from Act I
peach blouse
rust cardigan from Act I
green beads and locket from Act I
shoes from Act I

LAURIE

ACT I
  camisole, knickers
  beige argyle knee socks
  green jumper with red belt
  white blouse
  tan shoes

ACT II
  brown and tan checked dress
  gray knee socks
  shoes from Act I
  blue plaid bathrobe
  red striated stripe pullover sweater
  green jumper from Act I
  brown argyle knee socks
  shoes from Act I

ONSTAGE CHECK

ACT ONE

Dining table—marks
3 chairs pulled slightly away from table
On dining table
    Sewing machine w/material
    Sewing basket
    Top of sewing machine
    Fruit bowl
*Make sure latch and button are in right position to lock
      top.
*Beach chair s.l. w/glove, book, 3 white balls
Sideboard
Set out
    2 glasses
    3 shot glasses
    1 whiskey and 1 shot
    Pewter cream and sugar
In s.l. drawer
    7 napkins
    Extra pearls
    *2 dollar bills
In s.r. cabinet
    Lace table cloth
    Act 2—table cloth
In s.l. cabinet
    2 candlesticks
    2 candles
    7—Act 2—napkins
    Newspaper—Act 2
    Extra linen

On Sofa
  3 pillows
  Book
On floor DS. of sofa — *THE SOCK
Magazine rack — *newspaper — 2 sections
  Scrapbook
Mailbox — 4 letters w/Rosalyn Weiner #3*

KITCHEN CHECK
On Table
  Sliced bread on platter
  Butter dish
  Bowl w/beans and spoon
  Bowl w/applesauce and spoon
  7 plates w/lettuce
  Sugar bowl
  3 condiment plates — ketchup, mustard, pickles
  Saran wrapped bread — 7 slices covered w/2 plastic
    bags
On Sink
  6 dessert bowls
  4 cups and saucers
  Bowl w/applesauce, raisins and spoon
On Shelf above Sink
  2 cups & saucers
  Check for oatmeal cookies
On Floor under Sink
  Bucket
  Crash box
  *SKATE
Refrigerator
  Pitcher of lemonade
Laundry Basket

Bundle — w/apron
4 t-shirts
1 pair shorts
3 pair socks
On Stove
  Pot w/potatoes
  Coffee pot — check it has coffee in it
  Small teapot w/fresh hot tea
On Shelf above Stove
  One glass
  Small full water pitcher
On Floor under Stove
  Small tray w/dish, napkin, silver, glass
On Oven
  Large water pitcher — full
  2 glasses ½ full
  Tray w/7 glasses; 7 knives, forks and spoons
On Shelf above Oven
  Bowl w/snap beans
  2 extra glasses
On Ironing Board
Act One — table cloth
Upstairs
Blanche's room
  Medicine bottle at least ½ full
  Tablespoon
Girl's room
  Check for robe and towel — Jodi
  Check for robe and towel — Mandy
Boy's room
  Check for cigar box under bed w/coins and 4 stamps
  Top drawer w/at least 3 pencils, pads, penknife, report card
  2nd drawer w/2 sweaters, postcard

Prop table s.r.
  2 grocery bags
  Large bag
  Cream
  Stack mail
  2 small bags
  Yellow envelope w/letter
  1 small bag
  Loaf bread
  2 large boxes
  Check cousin Ed on top and cousin Sholem on bottom.
ACT TWO

Dining table moved to Act Two position
Fix chairs
Strike table cloth and fruit bowl
Set on sideboard
  *Candlesticks w/candles
  *7 napkins in s.l. drawer
Doublecheck for
  2 tablecloths
  Pearls
  Money
Put *Newspaper on beach chair and put chair in Act 2
    position
From living room strike to s.r. prop table
  *Green glass bowl
  3 letters
  Seashells
Put newspapers back in magazine rack
Put book back on sofa
Fix pillows on sofa
Upstairs
Blanche's room

Check *glasses in bag
Girl's room
　　Check it is straightened
Boy's room
　　Put *report card under pillow on Eugene's bed
　　Check Stanley's hat
　　Double check cigar box
When you see Elizabeth ask her if she has the pearls.
Kitchen
Table
　　Bread on platter
　　*Fruit bowl
　　Platter — w/7 slices bread
　　Beans & serving utensils
　　*7 plates
　　Bowl w/applesauce & spoon
Sink
　　1 glass ½ full water
Shelf above Stove:
　　Small water pitcher full
　　1 glass
Oven
　　Tray w/7 glasses, 7 knives, forks, spoons
　　Large water pitcher full
Shelf above Oven
　　Handful nuts
　　Extra glass
Shelf near Ironing Board
　　*Nut dish
Make sure dirty laundry has been removed from
　　washing machine.
IS WORK LITE OUT?*

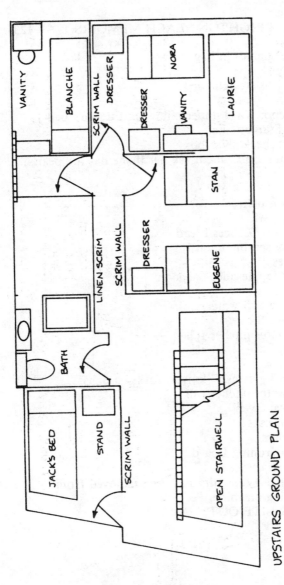

UPSTAIRS GROUND PLAN

SCENE DESIGN

" BRIGHTON BEACH MEMOIRS"

124

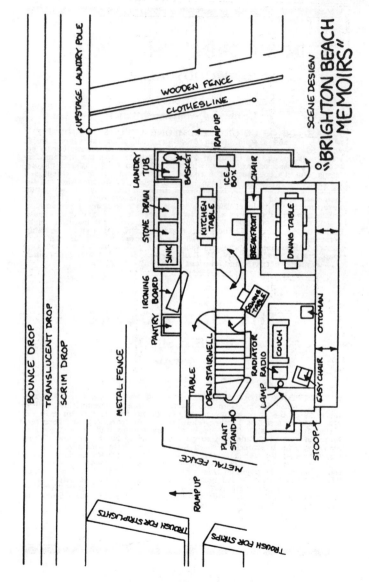

SCENE DESIGN
"BRIGHTON BEACH MEMOIRS"

BOUNCE DROP

TRANSLUCENT DROP

SCRIM DROP

METAL FENCE

UPSTAGE LAUNDRY POLE

WOODEN FENCE

CLOTHESLINE

RAMP UP

LAUNDRY TUB

STONE DRAIN

BASKET

ICE BOX

CHAIR

KITCHEN TABLE

SINK

BREAKFRONT

DINING TABLE

IRONING BOARD

PANTRY

IRONING TABLE

TABLE

OPEN STAIRWELL

RADIATOR

RADIO

COUCH

OTTOMAN

LAMP

EASY CHAIR

PLANT STAND

STOOP

METAL FENCE

RAMP UP

TROUGH FOR STRIP LIGHTS

TROUGH FOR STRIPS

125

DON'T DRINK THE WATER

By WOODY ALLEN

FARCE
12 men, 4 women—Interior

A CASCADE OF COMEDY FROM ONE OF OUR FUNNIEST CO-MEDIANS, and a solid hit on Broadway, this affair takes place inside an American embassy behind the Iron Curtain. An American tourist, caterer by trade, and his family of wife and daughter rush into the embassy two steps ahead of the police, who suspect them of spying and picture-taking. But it's not much of a refuge, for the ambassador is absent and his son, now in charge, has been expelled from a dozen countries and the whole continent of Africa. Nevertheless, they carefully and frantically plot their escape, and the ambassador's son and the caterer's daughter even have time to fall in love. "Because Mr. Allen is a working comedian himself, a number of the lines are perfectly agreeable . . . and there's quite a delectable bit of business laid out by the author and manically elaborated by the actor. . . . The gag is pleasantly outrageous and impeccably performed."—*N. Y. Times.* "Moved the audience to great laughter. . . . Allen's imagination is daffy, his sense of the ridiculous is keen and gags snap, crackle and pop."—*N. Y. Daily News.* "It's filled with funny lines. . . . A master of bright and hilarious dialogue."—*N. Y. Post.*

THE ODD COUPLE

By NEIL SIMON

COMEDY
6 men, 2 women—Interior

NEIL SIMON'S THIRD SUCCESS in a row begins with a group of the boys assembled for cards in the apartment of a divorced fellow, and if the mess of the place is any indication, it's no wonder that his wife left him. Late to arrive is another fellow who, they learn, has just been separated from his wife. Since he is very meticulous and tense, they fear he might commit suicide, and so go about locking all the windows. When he arrives, he is scarcely allowed to go to the bathroom alone. As life would have it, the slob bachelor and the meticulous fellow decide to bunk together—with hilarious results. The patterns of their own disastrous marriages begin to reappear in this arrangement; and so this too must end. "The richest comedy Simon has written and purest gold for any theatregoer. . . . This glorious play."—*N. Y. World-Telegram & Sun.* "His skill is not only great but constantly growing. . . . There is scarcely a moment that is not hilarious."—*N. Y. Times.*

The Gingerbread Lady

NEIL SIMON
(Little Theatre) Comedy-Drama
3 Men, 3 Women—Interior

Maureen Stapleton played the Broadway part of a popular singer who has gone to pot with booze and sex. We meet her at the end of a ten-week drying out period at a sanitarium, when her friend, her daughter, and an actor try to help her adjust to sobriety. But all three have the opposite effect on her. The friend is so constantly vain she loses her husband; the actor, a homosexual, is also doomed, and indeed loses his part three days before an opening; and the daughter needs more affection than she can spare her mother. Enter also a former lover louse, who ends up giving her a black eye. The birthday party washes out, the gingerbread lady falls off the wagon and careens onward to her own tragic end.

> "He has combined an amusing comedy with the atmosphere of great sadness. His characteristic wit and humor are at their brilliant best, and his serious story of lost misfits can often be genuinely and deeply touching."—N.Y. Post. "Contains some of the brightest dialogue Simon has yet composed."—N.Y. Daily News. "Mr. Simon's play is as funny as ever—the customary avalanche of hilarity, and landslide of pure unbuttoned joy . . . Mr. Simon is a funny, funny man—with tears running down his cheek."—N.Y. Times.

The Sunshine Boys

NEIL SIMON
(All Groups) Comedy
5 Men, 2 Women

An ex-vaudeville team, Al Lewis and Willie Clarke, in spite of playing together for forty-three years, have a natural antipathy for one another. (Willie resents Al's habit of poking a finger in his chest, or perhaps accidentally spitting in his face). It has been eleven years since they have performed together, when along comes CBS-TV, who is preparing a "History of Comedy" special, that will of course include Willie and Al—the "Lewis and Clark" team back together again. In the meantime, Willie has been doing spot commercials, like for Schick (the razor blade shakes) or for Frito-Lay potato chips (he forgets the name), while Al is happily retired. The team gets back together again, only to have Al poke his finger in Willie's chest, and accidentally spit in his face.

> ". . . the most delightful play Mr. Simon has written for several seasons and proves why he is the ablest current author of stage humor."—Watts, N. Y. Post. "None of Simon's comedies has been more intimately written out of love and a bone-deep affinity with the theatrical scene and temperament." Time. ". . . another hit for Neil Simon in this shrewdly balanced, splendidly performed and rather touching slice of the show-biz life."—Watt, New York Daily News. "(Simon) . . . writes the most dependably crisp and funny dialogue around . . . always well-set and polished to a high lustre."—WABC-TV. ". . . a vaudeville act within a vaudeville act . . . Simon has done it again."—WCBS-TV.

THE GOOD DOCTOR

NEIL SIMON

(All Groups) Comedy

2 Men, 3 Women. Various settings.

With Christopher Plummer in the role of the Writer, we are introduced to a composite of Neil Simon and Anton Chekhov, from whose short stories Simon adapted the capital vignettes of this collection. Frances Sternhagen played, among other parts, that of a harridan who storms a bank and upbraids the manager for his gout and lack of money. A father takes his son to a house where he will be initiated into the mysteries of sex, only to relent at the last moment, and leave the boy more perplexed than ever. In another sketch a crafty seducer goes to work on a wedded woman, only to realize that the woman has been in command from the first overture. Let us not forget the classic tale of a man who offers to drown himself for three rubles. The stories are droll, the portraits affectionate, the humor infectious, and the fun unending.

"As smoothly polished a piece of work as we're likely to see all season."—*N.Y. Daily News.* "A great deal of warmth and humor —vaudevillian humor—in his retelling of these Chekhovian tales."—*Newhouse Newspapers.* "There is much fun here . . . Mr. Simon's comic fancy is admirable."—*N.Y. Times.*

(Music available. Write for particulars.)

The Prisoner of Second Avenue

NEIL SIMON

(All Groups) Comedy

2 Men, 4 Women, Interior

Mel is a well-paid executive of a fancy New York company which has suddenly hit the skids and started to pare the payroll. Anxiety doesn't help; Mel, too, gets the ax. His wife takes a job to tide them over, then she too is sacked. As if this weren't enough, Mel is fighting a losing battle with the very environs of life. Polluted air is killing everything that grows on his terrace; the walls of the high-rise apartment are paper-thin, so that the private lives of a pair of German stewardesses next door are open books to him; the apartment is burgled; and his psychiatrist dies with $23,000 of his money. Mel does the only thing left for him to do: he has a nervous breakdown. It is on recovery that we come to esteem him all the more. For Mel and his wife and people like them have the resilience, the grit to survive.

"Now all this, mind you, is presented primarily in humorous terms."—*N.Y. Daily News.* "A gift for taking a grave subject and, without losing sight of its basic seriousness, treating it with hearty but sympathetic humor . . . A talent for writing a wonderfully funny line . . . full of humor and intelligence . . . Fine fun."—*N.Y. Post.* "Creates an atmosphere of casual cataclysm, and everyday urban purgatory of copelessness from which laughter seems to be released like vapor from the city's manholes."—*Time.*